STORIES FROM THE *Arabian Nights*

Laurence Housman

HAWK PRESS

Published by

Hawk Press
4836/24, Ansari Road, Daryaganj
New Delhi – 110 002
Phones : 9643330713, +91-11-23278618, +91-11-35676207
E-mail : thehawkpress@gmail.com
www.thehawkpress.com

ISBN : 978-93-95034-14-2

Contents

Scheherazadè, the heroine of the Thousand and One Nights.

PREFACE

Scheherazadè, the heroine of the Thousand and one Nights, ranks among the great story-tellers of the world much as does Penelope among the weavers. Procrastination was the basis of her art; for though the task she accomplished was splendid and memorable, it is rather in the quantity than the quality of her invention—in the long spun-out performance of what could have been done far more shortly—that she becomes a figure of dramatic interest. The idea which binds the stories together is greater and more romantic than the stories themselves; and though, both in the original and in translation, the diurnal interruption of their flow is more and more taken for granted, we are never quite robbed of the sense that it is Scheherazadè who is speaking—Scheherazadè, loquacious and self-possessed, sitting up in bed at the renewed call of dawn to save her neck for the round of another day. Here is a figure of romance worth a dozen of the prolix stories to which it has been made sponsor; and often we may have followed the fortunes of some shoddy hero and heroine chiefly to determine at what possible point of interest the narrator could have left hanging that frail thread on which for another twenty-four hours her life was to depend.

Yes, the idea is delightful; and, with the fiction of Scheherazadè to colour them, the tales acquire a rank which they would not otherwise deserve; their prolixity is then the crowning point of their art, their sententious truisms have a flavour of ironic wit, their repetitions become humorous, their trivialities a mark of light-hearted courage; even those deeper indiscretions, which Burton has so faithfully recorded, seem then but a wise adaptation of vile means to a noble end. And yet we know that it is not so; for, as a matter of fact, the "Arabian Nights Entertainment" is but a miscellany gathered from various sources, of various dates, and passing down to us, even in its collocated form, under widely differing versions. None but scholars can know how little of the unadulterated originals has come into our possession; and only those whose pious opinions shut their eyes to obvious facts can object in principle to the simplification of a form which, from the point of view of mere story-telling, can so easily be bettered. Even the more accurate of the versions ordinarily available are full of abridgement, alteration, and suppression; and if you have to eliminate Scheherazadè and select your stories mainly with a view to illustration, then you have very largely done away with the reasons for treating tenderly that prolixity which [Pg viii]in an impatient age tends to debar readers from an old classic.

And so, in the present version, whoever shall care to make comparison will find that the original material has been treated with considerable freedom in the direction of brevity, and with an almost uniform departure from the exact text, save where essentials of plot or character or local colour required a closer, accuracy. In the case also of conflicting versions, there has been no reluctance to choose and combine in order to secure a livelier result; and a further freedom has sometimes been taken of giving to an incident more meaning and connexion than has been allowed to it in the original. That is, perhaps, the greatest licence of all, but it is the one that does least harm in formal result; for no one can read the majority of the tales in their accepted versions without perceiving that, as regards construction and the piecing of event with event, they are either incredibly careless or discreditably perfunctory. We have to reckon with them as the product of a race keenly alive to the value of colour and pictorial description, but a race whose constructive imagination was feeble and diffuse, lacking almost entirely that great essential for the development of art in its finer forms—the economy of means toward ends.

But because they contain, though at a low pressure, the expression of so much life, habit and custom, so many coloured and secluded interiors, so quaint a commingling of crowds, so brilliant and moving a pageantry of Eastern mediævalism, because of all these things the "Arabian Nights" will still retain their perennial charm. Those of us who read are all travellers; and never is our travelling sense so awakened perhaps, as when we dip into a book such as this where the incredible and the common-place are so curiously blended, and where Jinn and Efreet and Magician have far less interest for us now than the silly staring crowds, and the bobbing camels in the narrow streets, and Scheherazadè spinning her poor thin yarn of wonders that she may share for another night the pillow of a homicidal maniac.

THE FISHERMAN AND THE GENIE

There was once an old fisherman who lived in great poverty with a wife and three children. But though poorer than others he ever toiled in humble submission to the decrees of Providence, and so, at the same hour each day, he would cast his net four times into the sea, and whatever it brought up to him therewith he rested content.

One day, having cast for the first time, he found his net so heavy that he could scarcely draw it in; yet when at last he got it to shore all that it contained was the carcase of an ass.

He cast a second time, and found the draught of the net even heavier than before. But again he was doomed to disappointment, for this time it contained nothing but a large earthenware jar full of mud and sand. His third attempt brought him only a heap of broken old bottles and potsherds: fortune seemed to be against him. Then, committing his hope to Providence, he cast for the fourth and last time; and once more the weight of the net was so great that he was unable to haul it. When at last he got it to land, he found that it contained a brazen vessel, its mouth closed with a leaden stopper, bearing upon it the seal of King Solomon.

The sight cheered him. "This," thought he, "I can sell in the market, where I may get for it enough to buy a measure of corn; and, if one is to judge by weight, what lies within may prove yet more valuable."

Thus reckoning, he prised out the stopper with his knife, and turning the vessel upside down looked for the contents to follow. Great was his astonishment when nothing but smoke came out of it. The smoke rose in a thick black column and spread like a mist between earth and sky, till presently, drawing together, it took form; and there in its midst stood a mighty Genie, whose brows touched heaven while his feet rested upon ground. His head was like a dome, his hands were like flails, and his legs like pine trees; his mouth was black as a cavern, his nostrils were like trumpets, his eyes blazed like torches, and his wings whirled round and over him like the simoom of the desert.

And there in its midst stood a mighty Genie.

At so fearful a sight all the fisherman's courage oozed out of him; but the Genie, perceiving him, cried with a loud voice, "O, Solomon, Prophet of God, slay me not, for never again will I withstand thee in word or deed!"

"Alas!" said the fisherman, "I am no prophet; and as for Solomon, he has been dead for nearly two thousand years. I am but a poor fisherman whom chance has knocked by accident against thy door."

"In that case," answered the Genie, "know that presently thou wilt have to die."

"Heaven forbid!" cried the fisherman; "or, at least, tell me why! Surely it might seem that I had done thee some service in releasing thee."

"Hear first my story," said the Genie, "then shalt thou understand."

"Well, if I must!" said the fisherman, resigning himself to the inevitable; "but make it short, for truly I have small stomach left in me now for the hearing of tales."

"Know, then," said the Genie, "that I am one of those spirits which resisted the power and dominion of Solomon; and when, having brought into submission all the rest of my race, he could not make me yield to him either reverence or service, he caused me to be shut up in this bottle, and sealing it with his own seal cast it down into the depths of the sea.

When having brought into submission all the rest of my race.

"Now when I had lain there prisoner for a hundred years, I swore in my heart that I would give to the man that should release me all the treasures attainable in heaven or earth. But when none came to earn so great a reward in all the hundred years that followed, then I swore that I would give to my liberator earthly riches only; and when this gift also had lain despised for yet another hundred years, then would I promise no more than the fulfilment of three wishes. But thereafter finding that all promises and vows were vain, my heart became consumed with rage, and I swore by Allah that I would only grant to the fool that should release me his own choice of the most cruel form of death by which he should die. Now therefore accept that mercy which I still offer and choose thy penalty!"

When the fisherman heard this he gave himself up for lost, yet he did not the less continue by prayer and supplication to entreat the Genie from his purpose. But when he found that there was no heart left in him to be moved, then for the first time he bestirred his wits, and remembering how that which is evil contains far less wisdom than that which is good, and so falls ever the more readily into the trap prepared for it, he spoke thus: "O Genie, since thou art determined on my death, there is yet a certain thing touching thine honour that I would first know. So, by the Ineffable Name, which is the seal of Solomon, I will ask thee one question, and do thou swear to answer it truly."

The Genie was ready enough to give the oath as desired. Then said the fisherman, "How is it that one so great as thou art, whose feet o'er-step the hills and whose head out-tops the heaven—how can such an one enter into so small a vessel to dwell in it? Truly, though mine eyes tell me I have seen it, I cannot any longer believe so great a marvel."

"What?" cried the Genie, "dost thou not believe what I have already told thee?"

"Not till I have seen it done can I believe it," said the fisherman.

Thereupon, without more waste of words, the Genie, drawing his limbs together and folding himself once more in a thick veil of smoke, descended from his vast altitude into the narrow neck of the brazen vessel till not one shred or film of him remained to view. Then the fisherman with a quick hand replaced the leaden stopper, and laughing, cried to the Genie, "Choose now, thou in thy turn, by what manner of death thou wilt die."

The Genie, hearing himself thus mocked, made violent efforts to escape; but the power of the seal of Solomon held him fast, and the fisherman, ceasing not all the while to revile him for the treachery and baseness which were now to receive their due reward, began to carry the vessel back to the sea's brink. "Now," said he, "thou shalt return to the place whence I drew thee! And here on the shore I will build myself a hut, and to every fisherman that comes near I will say, 'Look that you fish not in these waters, for herein lies bound a wicked genie that has sworn to put to a cruel death whoever dares to release him.'"

"Nay, nay," cried the Genie, "I did not mean what I said! Ask of me now, and I will give you all the treasures that the world contains, or that your heart can find in it to desire, if only you will set me free!"

The fisherman, being of a mild spirit and with no heart for revenge, sat down to consider what he should do, and all the while the imprisoned Genie continued to appeal to him for compassion with loud promise and lamentation. So at last, the fisherman, having the fear of God before his eyes, after he had extracted from the Genie a most solemn vow to leave him unharmed, drew out the stopper of lead and released him.

No sooner was he out and restored to his true form than the Genie, turning himself about, lifted his foot and with his full strength smote the brazen vessel far out to sea; and the fisherman, beholding that act, began to repent him of his mercy and to tremble again for dear life.

But the Genie, seeing his fear, broke into huge laughter, and striding on ahead of him cried, "Come, fisherman, and follow me, for now I will lead you to fortune!"

Meekly at his heels went the old fisherman, and leaving behind them the habitations of men they ascended a mountain and entered upon a desert tract guarded by four hills, in the centre of which lay a broad lake. Here the Genie stopped, and pointing to a place where fish were swimming in abundance bade the fisherman cast in his net. The fisherman did as he was told, and when he drew in his net he found that it contained four fish each of a different colour, a red, a white, a blue, and a yellow: never in his life had he seen the like of them. The Genie bade him take and offer them to the Sultan, assuring him that if he did so they should bring him both fortune and honours. Then he struck the ground with his foot, and immediately the earth opened its mouth and swallowed him as the dry desert swallows the rain.

The fisherman, wondering no less at his safe deliverance than at the marvel of these occurrences, made his way in haste to the city; and there presenting himself at the palace he begged that the four fish might be laid at the Sultan's feet, as a humble offering from the poorest of his subjects.

No sooner had the monarch seen them, so strange of form and so brilliant and diverse in hue, than his longing to taste of them became strongly awakened; so, by the hand of his Vizier, he sent them to the cook to be prepared forthwith for the royal table. As for the poor fisherman, he received no fewer than four hundred pieces of gold from the Sultan's bounty, and returned to his family rejoicing in an affluence which surpassed his utmost expectations.

No sooner had the monarch seen them, so strange of form and so brilliant and diverse in hue.

The cook meanwhile, proud of an opportunity to exhibit her culinary skill on dainties so rare, scaled and cleaned the fish and laid them in a frying-pan over the fire. But scarcely had she done so when the wall of the kitchen divided, and there issued forth from it a damsel of moon-like beauty richly apparelled, holding a rod of myrtle in her hand. With this she struck the fish that lay in the frying-pan, and cried—

"O fish of my pond,

Are ye true to your bond?"

And immediately the four fishes lifted their heads from the frying fat and answered—

"Even so, the bond holds yet;

Paid by thee, we pay the debt.

Whereupon one upset the pan into the fire.

With give and take is the reckoning met."

Thereupon the damsel upset the pan into the fire and retired through the wall in the same way that she had come, leaving the four fish all charred to a cinder.

The cook, beholding her labour thus brought to naught, began to weep and bewail herself, expecting no less than instant dismissal, and was still loud in her lamentations when the Vizier arrived to see if the fish were ready.

Recalling the fisherman by a swift messenger.

On hearing her account of what had occurred, the Vizier was greatly astonished, but feared to bring so strange a report to the Sultan's ears while the cravings of the royal appetite were still unsatisfied; so recalling the fisherman by a swift messenger, he bade him procure in all haste four more fish of the same kind, promising to reward him according to the speed with which he accomplished the task. So spurred, and by the additional favour of fortune, the fisherman fulfilled his mission in an astonishingly short space of time; but no sooner was the second lot of fish placed upon the fire in the Vizier's presence than once again the wall opened, and the damsel, appearing as before, struck the frying-pan with her rod, and cried—

"O fish of my pond,

Are ye true to your bond?"

And immediately the fish stood up on their tails in the frying fat and replied—

"Even so, the bond holds yet;

Paid by thee, we pay the debt.

With give and take is the reckoning met."

Whereupon she upset the pan into the fire and departed as she had come.

The Vizier, perceiving that so strange an event might no longer be kept from the royal knowledge, went and informed the Sultan of all that had occurred; and the monarch, as soon as he had heard the tale, now rendered more eager for the satisfaction of his eyes than he had previously been for the indulgence of his appetite, sent for the fisherman, and promised him yet another four hundred pieces of gold if he could within a given time procure four more fishes similar to those he had already brought on the previous occasions.

If the fisherman had been prompt at the Vizier's bidding, he made even greater speed to fulfil the royal command, and before the day was over—this time in the presence of the Sultan himself—four fish, of four diverse colours like to the first, were cleaned and laid into the pan ready for frying. But scarcely had they touched the fat when the wall opened in a clap like thunder, and there came forth with a face of rage a monstrous negro the size of a bull, holding in his hand the rod of myrtle. With this he struck the frying-pan, and cried in a terrible voice—

"O fish from the pond,

Are ye true to your bond?"

And when the fish had returned the same answer that the others had made before them, without more ado the negro overturned the pan upon the fire and departed as he had come.

When the Sultan's eyes had seen that marvel, he said to his Vizier, "Here is mystery set before us! Surely these fish that talk have a past and a history. Never shall I rest satisfied until I have learned it." So causing the fisherman to be brought before him, he inquired whence the fish came. The fisherman answered, "From a lake between four hills upon the mountain overlooking the city." The Sultan inquired how many days' journey it might be, and the fisherman replied that it was but a matter of a few hours going and returning. Then to the Sultan and his court it seemed that the old man was mocking them, for none had heard tell of any lake lying among the hills so near to that city; and the fisherman, seeing his word doubted, began to fear that the Genie was playing him a trick; for if the lake were now suddenly to vanish away, he might find his fortunes more undone at the end than at the beginning.

Yet the Sultan, though his Vizier and all his court sought to dissuade him, was firmly resolved on putting the matter to the proof; so he gave orders that an escort and camping tents should be immediately got ready, and, with the fisherman to guide, set forth to find the place that was told of.

And, sure enough, when they had ascended the mountain which all knew, they came upon a desert tract on which no man had previously set eyes; and there in its midst lay the lake filled with four kinds of fish, and beyond it stretched a vast and unknown country.

He arrived within sight of a palace of shining marble.

At this sight, so mysterious and unaccountable, of a strange region lying unbeknownst at the gates of his own capital, the monarch was seized with an overwhelming desire to press forward in solitary adventure to the discovery of its secret. To the cautious counsels of his Vizier he turned a deaf ear; but since it would not be safe for his subjects to know of his departure on an errand so perilous, it was given out that he had been stricken by sudden sickness. The door of the royal tent was closed, and at the dead of night the Sultan, admitting none but the Vizier into his confidence, set out secretly on his adventure.

Journeying by night and resting by day, he arrived on the third morning within sight of a palace of shining marble which, with its crowd of domes and minarets, stood solitary among the hills. No sign of life was about it, and when he drew near and knocked at the gates none came to answer him. Then, finding the doors unfastened, he took courage and entered; and advancing through chambers where gold lay as dust, and by fountains wherein pearls lay poured out like water, he found only solitude to greet him.

Wandering without aim among innumerable treasures unguarded and left to waste, the Sultan grew weary, and sat down in an embrasure to rest. Then it seemed to him that not far off he could hear a sorrowful voice chant verses of lamentation. Following the sounds with wonder he came to a curtained doorway, and passing through found himself in the presence of a fair youth richly dressed, seated upon a couch and bearing upon his countenance tokens of extreme grief and despondency. To the Sultan's proffered greeting the youth returned salutation, but did not stir from his seat. "Pardon me," he said, "for not rising; but my miserable condition makes it impossible." Having said this he again broke into doleful lamentation; and when the Sultan inquired as to the cause of so many tears, "See for yourself," he cried, "what I am now made into!" And lifting the skirt of his robe he revealed himself all stone from his waist to the soles of his feet, while from the waist upwards he was as other men. Then as he observed upon his visitor's countenance the expression of a lively curiosity and astonishment, "Doubtless," he went on, "as you now know the secret of my miserable condition you will wish also to hear my story." And he related it as follows:—

THE STORY OF THE KING OF THE EBONY ISLES

The Queen of the Ebony Isles.

"My father was king of the city which once stood about this palace. He was lord also of the Ebony Isles that are now the four hills which you passed on your way hither. When I succeeded to the throne upon his death, I took to wife my own cousin, the daughter of my uncle, with whom I lived for five years in the utmost confidence and felicity, continually entertained by the charm of her conversation and the beauty of her person, and happy in the persuasion that she found in me an equal satisfaction.

Supposing me asleep they began to talk.

"One day, however, it chanced, in the hour before dinner when the queen was gone to bathe and adorn herself, that I lay upon a couch beside which two female slaves sat fanning me; and they, supposing me to be asleep, began to talk concerning me and their mistress. 'Ah!' said one, 'how little our lord knows where our mistress goes to amuse herself every night while he lies dreaming!' 'How should he know?' returned the other, 'seeing that the cup of wine which she gives him each night contains a sleeping-draught, that causes him to sleep sound however long she is absent. Then at daybreak when she returns she burns perfumes under his nostrils, and he waking and finding her there guesses nothing. Pity it is that he cannot know of her treacherous ways, for surely it is a shame that a king's wife should go abroad and mix with base people.'

The cup of wine which she gives him each night contains a sleeping-draught.

"Now when I heard this the light of day grew dark before my eyes; but I lay on and made no sign, awaiting my wife's return. And she coming in presently, we sat down and ate and drank together according to custom; and afterwards, when I had retired and lain down, she brought me with her own hands the cup of spiced wine, inviting me to drink. Then I, averting myself, raised it to my lips, but instead of drinking, poured it by stealth into my bosom, and immediately sank down as though overcome by its potency, feigning slumber. Straightway the queen rose up from my side, and having clothed herself in gorgeous apparel and anointed herself with perfumes, she made her way secretly from the palace, and I with equal secrecy followed her.

"Soon, passing by way of the narrower streets, we arrived before the city gates; and immediately at a word from her the chains fell and the gates opened of their own accord, closing again behind us as soon as we had passed. At last she came to a ruined hut, and there entering I saw her presently with her veil laid aside, seated in familiar converse with a monstrous negro, the meanest and most vile of slaves, offering to him in abject servility dainties which she had carried from the royal table, and bestowing upon him every imaginable token of affection and regard.

"At this discovery I fell into a blind rage, and drawing my sword I rushed in and struck the slave from behind a blow upon the neck that should have killed him. Then believing that I had verily slain him, and before the queen found eyes to realize what had befallen, I departed under cover of night as quickly as I had come, and returned to the palace and my own chamber.

"On awaking the next morning I found the queen lying beside me as though nothing had happened, and at first I was ready to believe it had all been an evil dream; but presently I perceived her eyes red with weeping, her hair dishevelled, and her face torn by the passion of a grief which she strove to conceal. Having thus every reason to believe that my act of vengeance had not fallen short of its purpose, I held my tongue and made no sign.

"But the same day at noon, while I sat in council, the queen appeared before me clad in deep mourning, and with many tears informed me how she had received sudden news of the death of her father and mother and two brothers, giving full and harrowing details of each event. Without any show of incredulity I heard her tale; and when she besought my permission to go into retirement and mourn in a manner befitting so great a calamity, I bade her do as she desired.

"So for a whole year she continued to mourn in a privacy which I left undisturbed; and during that time she caused to be built a mausoleum or Temple of Lamentation—the same whose dome you see yonder—into which she withdrew herself from all society; while I, believing the cause of my anger removed and willing to humour the grief which my act had caused her, waited patiently for her return to a sane and reasonable state of mind.

"But, as I learned too late, matters had not so fallen: for though in truth the negro was grievously wounded, being cut through the gullet and speechless, it was not the will of Heaven that he should die; and the queen having by her enchantments kept him in a sort of life, no sooner was the mausoleum finished than she caused him to be secretly conveyed thither, and there night and day tended him, awaiting his full recovery.

She went on to vent her malice upon the city and islands.

"At length, when two years were over and her mourning in no wise abated, my curiosity became aroused; so going one day to the Temple of Lamentation I entered unannounced, and placing myself where I might see and not be seen, there I discovered her in an abandonment of fond weeping over her miserable treasure whose very life was a dishonour to us both. But no sooner in my just resentment had I started to upbraid her, than she—as now for the first time realizing the cause of her companion's misfortune—began to heap upon me terms of the most violent and shameful abuse; and when, carried beyond myself, I threatened her with my sword, she stood up before me, and having first uttered words of unknown meaning she cried,—

'Be thou changed in a moment's span;
Half be marble, and half be man!'

Began to heap upon me terms of the most violent and shameful abuse.

And at the word I became even as you see me now—dead to the waist, and above living yet bound. Yet even so her vengeance was not satisfied. Having reduced me to this state she went on to vent her malice upon the city and islands over which I ruled, and the unfortunate people who were my subjects. Thus by her wicked machinations the city became a lake, and the islands about it the four hills which you have seen; as for the inhabitants, who were of four classes and creeds, Moslems, Christians, Jews, and Persians, she turned them into fish of four different colours: the white are the Moslems, the red are Persian fire-worshippers, the yellow are Jews, and the blue Christians. And now having done all this she fails not every day to inflict upon me a hundred lashes with a whip which draws blood at every stroke: and when these are accomplished she covers my torn flesh with hair-cloth and lays over it these rich robes in mockery. Of a surety it is the will of Heaven that I should be the most miserable and despised of mortals!"

Thus by her wicked machinations the city became a lake.

Thus the youth finished his story, nor when he had ended could he refrain from tears. The Sultan also was greatly moved when he heard it, and his heart became full of a desire to avenge such injuries upon the doer of them. "Tell me," he said, "where is now this monster of iniquity?" "Sir," answered the youth, "I doubt not she is yonder in the mausoleum with her companion, for thither she goes daily so soon as she has measured out to me my full meed of chastisement: and as for this day my portion has been served to me, I am quit of her till tomorrow brings, the hour of fresh scourgings."

Now when this was told him the Sultan saw his way plain. "Be of good cheer," he said to the youth, "and endure with a quiet spirit yet once more the affliction she causes thee; for at the price of that single scourging I trust, by the will of Heaven, to set thee free."

So on the morrow the Sultan lay in close hiding until sounds reached him which told that the whippings had begun; then he arose and went in haste to the mausoleum, where amid rich hangings and perfumes and the illumination of a thousand candles, he found the black slave stretched mute upon a bed awaiting in great feebleness the recovered use of his sawn gullet. Quickly, with a single sword-stroke, the avenger took from him that poor remnant of life which enchantment alone had made possible: then having thrown the body into a well in the courtyard below, he lay down in the dead man's place, drawing the coverlet well over him. Soon after, fresh from her accustomed task of cruelty, the enchantress entered, and falling upon her knees beside the bed she cried, "Has my lord still no voice wherewith to speak to his servant? Surely, for lack of that sound, hearing lies withered within me!" Then the Sultan, taking to himself the thick speech of a negro, said, "There is no strength or power but in God alone!"

On hearing those words, believing that her companion's speech was at last restored to him, the queen uttered a cry of joy! But scarcely had she begun to lavish upon him the tokens of her affection when the pretended negro broke out against her in violent abuse. "What!" he cried, "dost thou expect favour at my hands, when it is because of thee that for two years I have lain dumb and prostrate? How darest thou speak to me or look for any recompense save death! Nay!" he went on in answer to her astonished protests, "have not the cries and tears and groans of thy husband kept me continually from rest: and has not

Heaven smitten me for no other reason than because thou wouldst not cease from smiting him? So has the curse which thou didst seek to lay upon him fallen doubly upon me."

"Alas!" cried the enchantress, "have I unknowingly caused thee so great an ill? If it be so, then let my lord give command, and whatever be his desire it shall be satisfied."

Then said the Sultan, "Go instantly and release thy husband from spell and torment: and when it is done, return hither with all speed."

Thus compelled, in great fear and bewilderment and sorely against her will, the queen sped to the chamber in the palace where her husband lay spell-bound. Taking a vessel of water she pronounced over it certain words which caused it instantly to boil as though it had been set on a fire: then throwing the water over him, she cried—

"Spell be loosed, and stone grow warm,

Yield back flesh to the human form."

And immediately on the word his nature came to him again, and he leaped and stood upon his feet. But the queen's hatred towards him was by no means abated. "Go hence quickly," she cried, "since a better will than mine releases thee! But if thou tarry or if thou return, thou shalt surely die!" Thankful for his deliverance the youth stayed not to question, but departing went and hid himself without, while the queen returned in haste to the mausoleum where her supposed lover awaited her. There, eager for restoration to favour, she informed him of what she had done, supposing that to be all.

"Nay," said the other, still speaking with the thick voice of a negro; "though thou hast lopped the branch of the evil thou hast not destroyed the root. For every night I hear a jumping of fishes in the lake that is between the four hills, and the sound of their curses on thee and me comes to disturb my rest. Go instantly and restore all things to their former state, then come back and give me thy hand and I shall rise up a sound man once more."

Rejoicing in that promise and the expectations it held out to her of future happiness, the queen went with all speed to the border of the lake. There taking a little water into her hand, and uttering strange words over it, she sprinkled it this way and that upon the surface of the lake and the roots of the four hills, and immediately where had been the lake a city appeared, and instead of fishes inhabitants, and in place of the four hills four islands. As for the palace it stood no longer removed far away into the desert but upon a hill overlooking the city.

Great was the astonishment of the Vizier and the Sultan's escort.

Great was the astonishment of the Vizier and the Sultan's escort which had lain encamped beside the lake to find themselves suddenly transported to the heart of a populous city, with streets and walls and the hum of reawakened life around them; but a greater and more terrible shock than this awaited the queen upon her return to the mausoleum to enjoy the reward of her labours. "Now," she cried, "let my lord arise, since all that he willed is accomplished!"

"Give me thy hand!" said the Sultan, still in a voice of disguise; "come nearer that I may lean on thee!" And as she approached he drew forth his sword which had lain concealed beside him in the bed, and with a single blow cleft her wicked body in twain.

Then he rose and went quickly to where in hiding lay the young king her husband, who learned with joy of the death of his cruel enemy. He thanked the Sultan with tears of gratitude for his deliverance, and invoked the blessings of Heaven upon him and his kingdom. "On yours too," said the Sultan, "let peace and prosperity now reign! And since your city is so near to mine, come with me and be my guest that we may rejoice together in the bonds of friendship."

"Nay," answered the young king, "tha· would I do willingly, but your country lies many a day's journey from my own. I fear the breaking of the spell which held me and my subjects has brought you further than you wished."

It was in fact true that the Ebony Isles had now returned to the place from which they had originally come. The Sultan put a smiling face upon the matter: "I can well put up with the tedium of my journey," said he, "if only you will be my companion. Nay, let me speak frankly to one whose demeanour in affliction has won my heart; I am childless and have no heir. Come with me and be my son, and when I am dead unite our two kingdoms under a single ruler." The young king, who had conceived for his deliverer an equal affection, could not withstand so noble and generous an offer: and so with a free exchange of hearts on both sides the matter was arranged.

After a journey of some months the Sultan arrived again at his own capital, where he was welcomed with great rejoicings by the people, who had long mourned over his strange and unexplained absence.

As for the old fisherman who had been the immediate cause of the young king's deliverance the Sultan loaded him with honours and gave his daughters in marriage to sons of the blood royal, so that they all continued in perfect happiness and contentment to the end of their days.

ALI BABA AND THE FORTY THIEVES

In a town in Persia lived two brothers named Cassim and Ali Baba, between whom their father at his death had left what little property he possessed equally divided. Cassim, however, having married the heiress of a rich merchant, became soon after his marriage the owner of a fine shop, together with several pieces of land, and was in consequence, through no effort of his own, the most considerable merchant in the town. Ali Baba, on the other hand, was married to one as poor as himself, and having no other means of gaining a livelihood he used to go every day into the forest to cut wood, and lading therewith the three asses which were his sole stock-in-trade, would then hawk it about the streets for sale.

One day while he was at work within the skirts of the forest, Ali Baba saw advancing towards him across the open a large company of horsemen, and fearing from their appearance that they might be robbers, he left his asses to their own devices and sought safety for himself in the lower branches of a large tree which grew in the close overshadowing of a precipitous rock.

Their chief in a low but distinct voice uttered the two words "Open Sesame!"

Almost immediately it became evident that this very rock was the goal toward which the troop was bound, for having arrived they alighted instantly from their horses, and took down each man of them a sack which seemed by its weight and form to be filled with gold. There could no longer be any doubt that they were robbers. Ali Baba counted forty of them.

Just as he had done so, the one nearest to him, who seemed to be their chief, advanced toward the rock, and in a low but distinct voice uttered the two words, "Open, Sesamé!" Immediately the rock opened like a door, the captain and his men passed in, and the rock closed behind them.

For a long while Ali Baba waited, not daring to descend from his hiding-place lest they should come out and catch him in the act; but at last, when the waiting had grown almost unbearable, his patience was rewarded, the door in the rock opened, and out came the forty men, their captain leading them. When the last of them was through, "Shut, Sesamé!" said the captain, and immediately the face of the rock closed together as before. Then they all mounted their horses and rode away.

As soon as he felt sure that they were not returning, Ali Baba came down from the tree and made his way at once to that part of the rock where he had seen the captain and his men enter. And there at the word "Open, Sesamé!" a door suddenly revealed itself and opened.

Ali Baba had expected to find a dark and gloomy cavern. Great was his astonishment therefore when he perceived a spacious and vaulted chamber lighted from above through a fissure in the rock; and there spread out before him lay treasures in profusion, bales of merchandise, silks, carpets, brocades, and above all gold and silver lying in loose heaps or in sacks piled one upon another. He did not take long to consider what he should do. Disregarding the silver and the gold that lay loose, he brought to the mouth of the cave as many sacks of gold as he thought his three asses might carry; and having loaded them on and covered them with wood so that they might not be seen, he closed the rock by the utterance of the magic words which he had learned, and departed for the town, a well-satisfied man.

When he got home he drove his asses into a small court, and shutting the gates carefully he took off the wood that covered the bags and carried them in to his wife. She, discovering them to be full of gold, feared that her husband had stolen them, and began sorrowfully to reproach him; but Ali Baba soon put her mind at rest on that score, and having poured all the gold into a great heap upon the floor he sat down at her side to consider how well it looked.

Ali Baba departed for the town a well satisfied man.

Soon his wife, poor careful body, must needs begin counting it over piece by piece. Ali Baba let her go on for awhile, but before long the sight set him laughing. "Wife," said he, "you will never make an end of it that way. The best thing to do is to dig a hole and bury it, then we shall be sure that it is not slipping through our fingers." "That will do well enough," said his wife, "but it would be better first to have the measure of it. So while you dig the hole I will go round to Cassim's and borrow a measure small enough to give us an exact reckoning." "Do as you will," answered her husband, "but see that you keep the thing secret."

Off went Ali Baba's wife to her brother-in-law's house. Cassim was from home, so she begged of his wife the loan of a small measure, naming for choice the smallest. This set the sister-in-law wondering. Knowing Ali Baba's poverty she was all the more curious to find out for what kind of grain so small a measure could be needed. So before bringing it she covered all the bottom with lard, and giving it to Ali Baba's wife told her to be sure and be quick in returning it. The other, promising to restore it punctually, made haste to get home; and there finding the hole dug for its reception she started to measure the money into it. First she set the measure upon the heap, then she filled it, then she carried it to the hole; and so she continued till the last measure was counted. Then, leaving Ali Baba to finish the burying, she carried back the measure with all haste to her sister-in-law, returning thanks for the loan.

No sooner was her back turned than Cassim's wife looked at the bottom of the measure, and there to her astonishment she saw sticking to the lard a gold coin. "What?" she cried, her heart filled with envy, "is Ali Baba so rich that he needs a measure for his gold? Where, then, I would know, has the miserable wretch obtained it?"

As soon as he came in she began to jeer at him.

She waited with impatience for her husband's return, and as soon as he came in she began to jeer at him. "You think yourself rich," said she, "but Ali Baba is richer. You count your gold by the piece, but Ali Baba does not count, he measures it! In comparison to Ali Baba we are but grubs and groundlings!"

Having thus riddled him to the top of her bent in order to provoke his curiosity, she told him the story of the borrowed measure, of her own stratagem, and of its result.

Cassim, instead of being pleased at Ali Baba's sudden prosperity, grew furiously jealous; not a wink could he sleep all night for thinking of it. The next morning before sunrise he went to his brother's house. "Ali Baba," said he, "what do you mean by pretending to be poor when all the time you are scooping up gold by the quart?" "Brother," said Ali Baba, "explain your meaning." "My meaning shall be plain!" cried Cassim, displaying the tell-tale coin. "How many more pieces have you like this that my wife found sticking to the bottom of the measure yesterday?"

Ali Baba, perceiving that the intervention of wives had made further concealment useless, told his brother the true facts of the case, and offered him, as an inducement for keeping the secret, an equal share of the treasure.

"That is the least that I have the right to expect," answered Cassim haughtily. "It is further necessary that you should tell me exactly where the treasure lies, that I may, if need be, test the truth of your story, otherwise I shall find it my duty to denounce you to the authorities."

Ali Baba, having a clear conscience, had little fear of Cassim's threats; but out of pure good nature he gave him all the information he desired, not forgetting to instruct him in the words which would give him free passage into the cave and out again.

Cassim, who had thus secured all he had come for, lost no time in putting his project into execution. Intent on possessing himself of all the treasures which yet remained, he set off the next morning before daybreak, taking with him ten mules laden with empty crates. Arrived before the cave, he recalled the words which his brother had taught him; no sooner was "Open, Sesamé!" said than the door in the rock lay wide for him to pass through, and when he had entered it shut again.

If the simple soul of Ali Baba had found delight in the riches of the cavern, greater still was the exultation of a greedy nature like Cassim's. Intoxicated with the wealth that lay before his eyes, he had no thought but to gather together with all speed as much treasure as the ten mules could carry; and so, having exhausted himself with heavy labour and avaricious excitement, he suddenly found on returning to the door that he had forgotten the key which opened it. Up and down, and in and out through the mazes of his brain he chased the missing ord. Barley, and maize, and rice, he thought of them all: but of sesamé never once, because his mind had become dark to the revealing light of heaven. And so the door stayed fast, holding him prisoner in the cave, where to his fate, undeserving of pity, we leave him.

Greater still was the exultation of a greedy nature like that of Cassim's.

Toward noon the robbers returned, and saw, standing about the rock, the ten mules laden with crates. At this they were greatly surprised, and began to search with suspicion amongst the surrounding crannies and undergrowth. Finding no one there, they drew their swords and advanced cautiously toward the cave, where, upon the captain's pronouncement of the magic word, the door immediately fell open. Cassim, who from within had heard the trampling of horses, had now no doubt that the robbers were arrived and that his hour was come. Resolved however to make one last effort at escape, he stood ready by the door; and no sooner had the opening word been uttered than he sprang forth with such violence that he threw the captain to the ground. But his attempt was vain; before he could break through he was mercilessly hacked down by the swords of the robber band.

With their fears thus verified, the robbers anxiously entered the cave to view the traces of its late visitant. There they saw piled by the door the treasure which Cassim had sought to carry away; but while restoring this to its place they failed altogether to detect the earlier loss which Ali Baba had caused them. Reckoning, however, that as one had discovered the secret of entry others also might know of it, they determined to leave an example for any who might venture thither on a similar errand; and having quartered the body of Cassim they disposed it at the entrance in a manner most calculated to strike horror into the heart of the beholder. Then, closing the door of the cave, they rode away in the search of fresh exploits and plunder.

Meanwhile Cassim's wife had grown very uneasy at her husband's prolonged absence; and at nightfall, unable to endure further suspense, she ran to Ali Baba, and telling him of his brother's secret expedition, entreated him to go out instantly in search of him.

Ali Baba had too kind a heart to refuse or delay comfort to her affliction. Taking with him his three asses he set out immediately for the forest, and as the road was familiar to him he had soon found his way to the door of the cave. When he saw there the traces of blood he became filled with misgiving, but no sooner had he entered than his worst fears were realized. Nevertheless brotherly piety gave him courage. Gathering together the severed remains and wrapping them about with all possible decency, he laid them upon one of the asses; then bethinking him that he deserved some payment for his pains, he loaded the two remaining asses with sacks of gold, and covering them with wood as on the first occasion, made his way back to the town while it was yet early. Leaving his wife to dispose of the treasure borne by the two asses, he led the third to his sister-in-law's house, and knocking quietly so that none of the neighbours might hear, was presently admitted by Morgiana, a female slave whose intelligence and discretion had long been known to him. "Morgiana," said he, "there's trouble on the back of that ass. Can you keep a secret?" And Morgiana's nod satisfied him better than any oath. "Well," said he, "your master's body lies there waiting to be pieced, and our business now is to bury him honourably as though he had died a natural death. Go and tell your mistress that I want to speak to her."

Mustapha doubted much of his ability to refrain from question.

Morgiana went in to her mistress, and returning presently bade Ali Baba enter. Then, leaving him to break to his sister-in-law the news and the sad circumstances of his brother's death, she, with her plan already formed, hastened forth and knocked at the door of the nearest apothecary. As soon as he opened to her she required of him in trembling agitation certain pillules efficacious against grave disorders, declaring in answer to his questions that her master had been taken suddenly ill. With these she returned home, and her plan of concealment having been explained and agreed upon much to the satisfaction of Ali Baba, she went forth the next morning to the same apothecary, and with tears in her eyes besought him to supply her in haste with a certain drug that is given to sick people only in the last extremity. Meanwhile the rumour of Cassim's sickness had got abroad; Ali Baba and his wife had been seen coming and going, while Morgiana by her ceaseless activity had made the two days' pretended illness seem like a fortnight: so when a sound of wailing arose within the house all the neighbours concluded without further question that Cassim had died a natural and honourable death.

But Morgiana had now a still more difficult task to perform, it being necessary for the obsequies that the body should be made in some way presentable. So at a very early hour the next morning she went to the shop of a certain merry old cobbler, Baba Mustapha by name, who lived on the other side of the town. Showing him a piece of gold she inquired whether he were ready to earn it by exercising his craft in implicit obedience to her instructions. And when Baba Mustapha sought to know the terms, "First," said she, "you must come with your eyes bandaged; secondly, you must sew what I put before you without asking questions; and thirdly, when you return you must tell nobody."

This way and that she led him blindfold.

Mustapha, who had a lively curiosity into other folk's affairs, boggled for a time at the bandaging, and doubted much of his ability to refrain from question; but having on these considerations secured the doubling of his fee, he promised secrecy readily enough, and taking his cobbler's tackle in hand submitted himself to Morgiana's guidance and set forth. This way and that she led him blindfold, till she had brought him to the house of her deceased master. Then uncovering his eyes in the presence of the dismembered corpse, she bade him get out thread and wax and join the pieces together.

Baba Mustapha plied his task according to the compact, asking no question. When he had done, Morgiana again bandaged his eyes and led him home, and giving him a third piece of gold the more to satisfy him, she bade him good-day and departed.

So in seemliness and without scandal of any kind were the obsequies of the murdered Cassim performed. And when all was ended, seeing that his widow was desolate and his house in need of a protector, Ali Baba with brotherly piety took both the one and the other into his care, marrying his sister-in-law according to Moslem rule, and removing with all his goods and newly acquired treasure to the house which had been his brother's. And having also acquired the shop where Cassim had done business, he put into it his own son, who had already served an apprenticeship to the trade. So, with his fortune well established, let us now leave Ali Baba and return to the robbers'cave.

Thither, at the appointed time, came the forty robbers, bearing in hand fresh booty; and great was their consternation to discover that not only had the body of Cassim been removed, but a good many sacks of gold as well. It was no wonder that this should trouble them, for so long as any one could command secret access, the cave was useless as a depository for their wealth. The question was, What could they do to put an end to their present insecurity? After long debate it was agreed that one of their number should go into the town disguised as a traveller, and there, mixing with the common people, learn from their report whether there had been recently any case in their midst of sudden prosperity or sudden death. If such a thing could be discovered, then they made sure of tracking the evil to its source and imposing a remedy.

Although the penalty for failure was death, one of the robbers at once boldly offered himself for the venture, and having transformed himself by disguise and received the wise counsels and commendations of his fellows, he set out for the town.

Having transformed himself by disguise.

Arriving at dawn he began to walk up and down the streets and watch the early stirring of the inhabitants. So, before long, he drew up at the door of Baba Mustapha, who, though old, was already seated at work upon his cobbler's bench. The robber accosted him. "I wonder," said he, "to see a man of your age at work so early. Does not so dull a light strain your eyes?" "Not so much as you might think," answered Baba Mustapha. "Why, it was but the other day that at this same hour I saw well enough to stitch up a dead body in a place where it was certainly no lighter." "Stitch up a dead body!" cried the robber, in pretended amazement, concealing his joy at this sudden intelligence. "Surely you mean in its winding sheet, for how else can a dead body be stitched?" "No, no," said Mustapha; "what I say I mean; but as it is a secret, I can tell you no more." The robber drew out a piece of gold. "Come," said he, "tell me nothing you do not care to; only show me the house where lay the body that you stitched." Baba Mustapha eyed the gold longingly. "Would that I could," he replied; "but alas! I went to it blindfold." "Well," said the robber, "I have heard that a blind man remembers his road; perhaps, though seeing you might lose it, blindfold you might find it again." Tempted by the offer of a second piece of gold, Baba Mustapha was soon persuaded to make the attempt. "It was here that I started," said he, showing the spot, "and I turned as you see me now." The robber then put a bandage over his eyes, and walked beside him through the streets, partly guiding and partly being led, till of his own accord Baba Mustapha stopped. "It was here," said he. "The door by which I went in should now lie to the right." And he had in fact come exactly opposite to the house which had once been Cassim's, where Ali Baba now dwelt.

The robber, having marked the door with a piece of chalk which he had provided for the purpose, removed the bandage from Mustapha's eyes, and leaving him to his own devices returned with all possible speed to the cave where his comrades were awaiting him.

Soon after the robber and cobbler had parted, Morgiana happened to go out upon an errand, and as she returned she noticed the mark upon the door. "This," she thought, "is not as it should be; either some trick is intended, or there is evil brewing for my masters house." Taking a piece of chalk she put a similar mark upon the five or six doors lying to right and left; and having done this she went home with her mind satisfied, saying nothing.

In the meantime the robbers had learned from their companion the success of his venture. Greatly elated at the thought of the vengeance so soon to be theirs, they formed a plan for entering the city in a manner that should arouse no suspicion among the inhabitants. Passing in by twos and threes, and by different routes, they came together to the market-place at an appointed time, while the captain and the robber who had acted as spy made their way alone to the street in which the marked door was to be found. Presently, just as they had expected, they perceived a door with the mark on it. "That is it!" said the robber; but as they continued walking so as to avoid suspicion, they came upon another and another, till, before they were done, they had passed six in succession. So alike were the marks that the spy, though he swore he had made but one, could not tell which it was. Seeing that the design had failed, the captain returned to the market-place, and having passed the word for his troop to go back in the same way as they had come, he himself set the example of retreat.

When they were all reassembled in the forest, the captain explained how the matter had fallen, and the spy, acquiescing in his own condemnation, kneeled down and received the stroke of the executioner.

But as it was still necessary for the safety of all that so great a trespass and theft should not pass unavenged, another of the band, undeterred by the fate of his comrade, volunteered upon the same conditions to prosecute the quest wherein the other had failed. Coming by the same means to the house of Ali Baba, he set upon the door, at a spot not likely to be noticed, a mark in red chalk to distinguish it clearly from those which were already marked in white. But even this precaution failed of its end. Morgiana, whose eye nothing could escape, noticed the red mark at the first time of passing, and dealt with it just as she had done with the previous one. So when the robbers came, hoping this time to light upon the door without fail, they found not one but six, all similarly marked with red.

When the second spy had received the due reward of his blunder, the captain considered how by trusting to others he had come to lose two of his bravest followers, so the third attempt he determined to conduct in person. Having found his way to Ali Baba's door, as the two others had done by the aid of Baba Mustapha, he did not set any mark upon it, but examined it so carefully that he could not in future mistake it. He then returned to the forest and communicated to his band the plan which he had formed. This was to go into the town in the disguise of an oil-merchant, bearing with him upon nineteen mules thirty-eight large leather jars, one of which, as a sample, was to be full of oil, but all the others empty. In these he purposed to conceal the thirty-seven robbers to which his band was now reduced, and so to convey his full force to the scene of action in such a manner as to arouse no suspicion till the signal for vengeance should be given.

Within a couple of days he had secured all the mules and jars that were requisite, and having disposed of his troop according to the pre-arranged plan, he drove his train of well-laden mules to the gates of the city, through which he passed just before sunset. Proceeding thence to Ali Baba's house, and arriving as it fell dark, he was about to knock and crave a lodging for the night, when he perceived Ali Baba at the door enjoying the fresh air after supper. Addressing him in tones of respect, "Sir," said he, "I have brought my oil a great distance to sell to-morrow in the market; and at this late hour, being a stranger, I know not where to seek for a shelter. If it is not troubling you too much, allow me to stable my beasts here for the night."

"Sir," said he, "I have brought my oil a great distance to sell to-morrow."

The captain's voice was now so changed from its accustomed tone of command, that Ali Baba, though he had heard it before, did not recognize it. Not only did he grant the stranger's request for bare accommodation, but as soon as the unlading and stabling of the mules had been accomplished, he invited him to stay no longer in the outer court but enter the house as his guest. The captain, whose plans this proposal somewhat disarranged, endeavoured to excuse himself from a pretended reluctance to give trouble; but since Ali Baba would take no refusal he was forced at last to yield, and to submit with apparent complaisance to an entertainment which the hospitality of his host extended to a late hour.

When they were about to retire for the night, Ali Baba went into the kitchen to speak to Morgiana; and the captain of the robbers, on the pretext of going to look after his mules, slipped out into the yard where the oil jars were standing in line. Passing from jar to jar he whispered into each, "When you hear a handful of pebbles fall from the window of the chamber where I am lodged, then cut your way out of the jar and make ready, for the time will have come." He then returned to the house, where Morgiana came with a light and conducted him to his chamber.

Now Ali Baba, before going to bed, had said to Morgiana, "To-morrow at dawn I am going to the baths; let my bathing-linen be put ready, and see that the cook has some good broth prepared for me against my return." Having therefore led the guest up to his chamber, Morgiana returned to the kitchen and ordered Abdallah the cook to put on the pot for the broth. Suddenly while she was skimming it, the lamp went out, and, on searching, she found there was no more oil in the house. At so late an hour no shop would be open, yet somehow the broth had to be made, and that could not be done without a light. "As for that," said Abdallah, seeing her perplexity, "why trouble yourself? There is plenty of oil out in the yard." "Why, to be sure!" said Morgiana, and sending Abdallah to bed so that he might be up in time to wake his master on the morrow, she took the oil-can herself and went out into the court. As she approached the jar which stood nearest, she heard a voice within say, "Is it time?"

To one of Morgiana's intelligence an oil-jar that spoke was an object of even more suspicion than a chalk-mark on a door, and in an instant she apprehended what danger for her master and his family might lie concealed around her. Understanding well enough that an oil-jar which asked a question required an answer, she replied quick as thought and without the least sign of perturbation, "Not yet, but presently." And thus she passed from jar to jar, thirty-seven in all, giving the same answer, till she came to the one which contained the oil.

The situation was now clear to her. Aware of the source from which her master had acquired his wealth, she guessed at once that, in extending shelter to the oil-merchant, Ali Baba had in fact admitted to his house the robber captain and his band. On the instant her resolution was formed. Having filled the oil-can she returned to the kitchen; there she lighted the lamp, and then, taking a large kettle, went back once more to the jar which contained the oil. Filling the kettle she carried it back to the kitchen, and putting under it a great fire of wood had soon brought it to the boil. Then taking it in hand once more, she went out into the yard and poured into each jar in turn a sufficient quantity of the boiling oil to scald its occupant to death.

She then returned to the kitchen, and having made Ali Baba's broth, put out the fire, blew out the lamp, and sat down by the window to watch.

She poured into each jar in turn a sufficient quantity of the boiling oil to scald its occupant to death.

Before long the captain of the robbers awoke from the short sleep which he had allowed himself, and finding that all was silent in the house, he rose softly and opened the window. Below stood the oil-jars; gently into their midst he threw the handful of pebbles agreed on as a signal; but from the oil-jars came no answer. He threw a second and a third time; yet though he could hear the pebbles falling among the jars, there followed only the silence of the dead. Wondering whether his band had fled leaving him in the lurch, or whether they were all asleep, he grew uneasy, and descending in haste, made his way into the court. As he approached the first jar a smell of burning and hot oil assailed his nostrils, and looking within he beheld in rigid contortion the dead body of his comrade. In every jar the same sight presented itself till he came to the one which had contained the oil. There, in what was missing, the means and manner of his companions' death were made clear to him. Aghast at the discovery and awake to the danger that now threatened him, he did not delay an instant, but forcing the garden-gate, and thence climbing from wall to wall, he made his escape out of the city.

When Morgiana, who had remained all this time on the watch, was assured of his final departure, she put her master's bath-linen ready, and went to bed well satisfied with her day's work.

The next morning Ali Baba, awakened by his slave, went to the baths before daybreak. On his return he was greatly surprised to find that the merchant was gone, leaving his mules and oil-jars behind him. He inquired of Morgiana the reason. "You will find the reason," said she, "if you look into the first jar you come to." Ali Baba did so, and, seeing a man, started back with a cry. "Do not be afraid," said Morgiana, "he is dead and harmless; and so are all the others whom you will find if you look further."

As Ali Baba went from one jar to another, finding always the same sight of horror within, his knees trembled under him; and when he came at last to the one empty oil-jar, he stood for a time motionless, turning upon Morgiana eyes of wonder and inquiry. "And what," he said then, "has become of the merchant?" "To tell you that," said Morgiana, "will be to tell you the whole story; you will be better able to hear it if you have your broth first."

When Morgiana who had remained all this time on the watch.

But the curiosity of Ali Baba was far too great: he would not be kept waiting. So without further delay she gave him the whole history, so far as she knew it, from beginning to end; and by her intelligent putting of one thing against another, she left him at last in no possible doubt as to the source and nature of the conspiracy which her quick wits had so happily defeated. "And now, dear master," she said in conclusion, "continue to be on your guard, for though all these are dead, one remains alive; and he, if I mistake not, is the captain of the band, and for that reason the more formidable and the more likely to cherish the hope of vengeance."

When Morgiana had done speaking Ali Baba clearly perceived that he owed to her not merely the protection of his property but life itself.

His heart was full of gratitude. "Do not doubt," he said, "that before I die I will reward you as you deserve; and as an immediate proof from this moment I give you your liberty."

This token of his approval filled Morgiana's heart with delight, but she had no intention of leaving so kind a master, even had she been sure that all danger was now over. The immediate question which next presented itself was how to dispose of the bodies. Luckily at the far end of the garden stood a thick grove of trees, and under these Ali Baba was able to dig a large trench without attracting the notice of his neighbours. Here the remains of the thirty-seven robbers were laid side by side, the trench was filled again, and the ground made level. As for the mules, since Ali Baba had no use for them, he sent them, one or two at a time, to the market to be sold.

Meanwhile the robber captain had fled back to the forest. Entering the cave he was overcome by its gloom and loneliness. "Alas!" he cried, "my comrades, partners in my adventures, sharers of my fortune, how shall I endure to live without you? Why did I lead you to a fate where valour was of no avail, and where death turned you into objects of ridicule? Surely had you died sword in hand my sorrow had been less bitter! And now what remains for me but to take vengeance for your death and to prove, by achieving it without aid, that I was worthy to be the captain of such a band!"

Thus resolved, at an early hour the next day, he assumed a disguise suitable to his purpose, and going to the town took lodging in a khan. Entering into conversation with his host he inquired whether anything of interest had happened recently in the town; but the other, though full of gossip, had nothing to tell him concerning the matter in which he was most interested, for Ali Baba, having to conceal from all the source of his wealth, had also to be silent as to the dangers in which it involved him.

The captain then inquired where there was a shop for hire; and hearing of one that suited him, he came to terms with the owner, and before long had furnished it with all kinds of rich stuffs and carpets and jewelry which he brought by degrees with great secrecy from the cave.

Now this shop happened to be opposite to that which had belonged to Cassim and was now occupied by the son of Ali Baba; so before long the son and the new-comer, who had assumed the name of Cogia Houssain, became acquainted; and as the youth had good looks, kind manners, and a sociable disposition, it was not long before the acquaintance became intimate.

Cogia Houssain did all he could to seal the pretended friendship, the more so as it had not taken him long to discover how the young man and Ali Baba were related; so, plying him constantly with small presents and acts of hospitality, he forced on him the obligation of making some return.

Ali Baba's son, however, had not at his lodging sufficient accommodation for entertainment; he therefore told his father of the difficulty in which Cogia Houssain's favours had placed him, and Ali Baba with great willingness at once offered to arrange matters. "My son," said he, "to-morrow being a holiday, all shops will be closed; then do you after dinner invite Cogia Houssain to walk with you; and as you return bring him this way and beg him to come in. That will be better than a formal invitation, and Morgiana shall have a supper prepared for you."

This proposal was exactly what Ali Baba's son could have wished, so on the morrow he brought Cogia Houssain to the door as if by accident, and stopping, invited him to enter.

Cogia Houssain, who saw his object thus suddenly attained, began by showing pretended reluctance, but Ali Baba himself coming to the door, pressed him in the most kindly manner to enter, and before long had conducted him to the table, where food stood prepared.

But there an unlooked-for difficulty arose. Wicked though he might be the robber captain was not so impious as to eat the salt of the man he intended to kill. He therefore began with many apologies to excuse himself; and when Ali Baba sought to know the reason, "Sir," said he, "I am sure that if you knew the cause of my resolution you would approve of it. Suffice it to say that I have made it a rule to eat of no dish that has salt in it. How then can I sit down at your table if I must reject everything that is set before me?"

"If that is your scruple," said Ali Baba, "it shall soon be satisfied," and he sent orders to the kitchen that no salt was to be put into any of the dishes presently to be served to the newly arrived guest. "Thus," said he to Cogia Houssain, "I shall still have the honour, to which I have looked forward, of returning to you under my own roof the hospitality you have shown to my son." Morgiana, who was just about to serve supper, received the order with some discontent. "Who," she said, "is this difficult person that refuses to eat salt? He must be a curiosity worth looking at." So when the saltless courses were ready to be set upon the table, she herself helped to carry in the dishes. No sooner had she set eyes on Cogia Houssain than she recognized him in spite of his disguise; and observing his movements with great attention she saw that he had a dagger concealed beneath his robe. "Ah!" she said to herself, "here is reason enough! For who will eat salt with the man he means to murder? But he shall not murder my master if I can prevent it."

Now Morgiana knew that the most favourable opportunity for the robber captain to carry out his design would be after the courses had been withdrawn, and when Ali Baba and his son and guest were alone together over their wine, which indeed was the very project that Cogia Houssain had formed. Going forth, therefore, in haste, she dressed herself as a dancer, assuming the headdress and mask suitable for the character. Then she fastened a silver girdle about her waist, and hung upon it a dagger of the same material. Thus equipped, she said to Abdallah the cook, "Take your tabor and let us go in and give an entertainment in honour of our master's guest."

So Abdallah took his tabor, and played Morgiana into the hall. As soon as she had entered she made a low curtsey, and stood awaiting orders. Then Ali Baba, seeing that she wished to perform in his guest's honour, said kindly, "Come in, Morgiana, and show Cogia Houssain what you can do."

Immediately Abdallah began to beat upon his tabor and sing an air for Morgiana to dance to; and she, advancing with much grace and propriety of deportment, began to move through several figures, performing them with the ease and facility which none but the most highly practised can attain to. Then, for the last figure of all, she drew out the dagger and, holding it in her hand, danced a dance which excelled all that had preceded it in the surprise and change and quickness and dexterity of its movements. Now she presented the dagger at her own breast, now at one of the onlookers; but always in the act of striking she drew back. At length, as though out of breath, she snatched his instrument from

Abdallah with her left hand, and, still holding the dagger in her right, advanced the hollow of the tabor toward her master, as is the custom of dancers when claiming their fee. Ali Baba threw in a piece of gold; his son did likewise. Then advancing it in the same manner toward Cogia Houssain, who was feeling for his purse, she struck under it, and before he knew had plunged her dagger deep into his heart.

Then for the last figure of all she drew out the dagger.

Ali Baba and his son, seeing their guest fall dead, cried out in horror at the deed. "Wretch!" exclaimed Ali Baba, "what ruin and shame hast thou brought on us?" "Nay," answered Morgiana, "it is not your ruin but your life that I have thus secured; look and convince yourself what man was this which refused to eat salt with you!" So saying, she tore off the dead robbers disguise, showing the dagger concealed below, and the face which her master now for the first time recognized.

Ali Baba's gratitude to Morgiana for thus preserving his life a second time, knew no bounds. He took her in his arms and embraced her as a daughter. "Now," said he, "the time is come when I must fulfil my debt; and how better can I do it than by marrying you to my son?" This proposition, far from proving unwelcome to the young man, did but confirm an inclination already formed. A few days later the nuptials were celebrated with great joy and solemnity, and the union thus auspiciously commenced was productive of as much happiness as lies within the power of mortals to secure.

As for the robbers'cave, it remained the secret possession of Ali Baba and his posterity; and using their good fortune with equity and moderation, they rose to high office in the city and were held in great honour by all who knew them.

THE STORY OF THE MAGIC HORSE

In the land of the Persians there lived in ancient times a King who had three daughters and an only son of such beauty that they drew the eyes of all beholders like moonrise in a clear heaven. Now it was the custom in that country for a great festival to be held at the new year, during which people of all grades, from the highest to the lowest, presented themselves before the King with offerings and salutations. So it happened that on one of these days there came to the King as he sat in state three sages, masters of their craft, bringing gifts for approval. The first had with him a peacock of gold which was so constructed that at the passing of each hour it beat its wings and uttered a cry. And the King, having proved it, found the gift acceptable and caused the inventor thereof to be suitably rewarded. The second had made a trumpet so that if placed over the gates of a city it blew a blast against any that sought to enter; and thus was the city held safe from surprise by an enemy. And when the King had found that it possessed that property, he accepted it, bestowing on its maker a rich reward.

But the gift of the third sage, who was an Indian, appeared more prodigious than all, for he had brought with him a horse of ivory and ebony, for which he claimed that, at the will of its owner, or of any one instructed in the secret, it would rise above the earth and fly, arriving at distant places in a marvellously short space of time. The King, full of wonder at such a statement, and eager to test it, was in some doubt as to how he might do so, for the Indian was unwilling to part with the secret until secure of the reward which in his own mind he had fixed on. Now it happened that at a distance of some three leagues from the city there stood a mountain the top of which was clearly discernible to all eyes; so, in order that the Indian's word might be proved, the King, pointing to it, said, "Go yonder, and bring back to me while I wait the branch of a palm-tree which grows at the foot of that mountain; then I shall know that what you tell me is true."

Instantly the Indian set foot in the stirrup and vaulted upon his charger, and scarcely had he turned a small peg which was set in the pommel of the saddle, when the horse rose lightly into the air and bore him away at wondrous speed amid the shouts of the beholders; and while all were still gazing, amazed at so sudden a vanishing, he reappeared high overhead, bearing the palm branch, and descending into their midst alighted upon the very spot from which he had started, where, prostrating himself, he laid the branch at the King's feet.

At so arrogant a claim all the courtiers burst into loud laughter.

The King was so delighted when the wonderful properties of the horse had been thus revealed to him, that, eager to possess it, he bade the Indian name his own reward, declaring that no price could be too great. Then said the sage, "Since your Majesty so truly appreciates the value of my invention, I do not fear that the reward I ask for will seem too high. Give me in marriage the hand of the fairest of your three daughters, and the horse shall be yours."

At so arrogant a claim all the courtiers burst into loud laughter; the King alone, consumed with the desire of possessing the wonderful treasure, hesitated as to what answer he should give. Then the King's son, Prince Firouz Schah, seeing his father lend ear to so shameful a proposal, became moved with indignation. Determined to defend his sister's honour and his own, he addressed the King. "Pardon me, Sire," said he, "if I take the liberty of speaking. But how shall it be possible for one of the greatest and most powerful monarchs to ally himself to a mere nobody? I entreat you to consider what is due not to yourself alone but to the high blood of your ancestors and of your children."

"My son," replied the King of Persia, "what you say is very true, so far as it goes; but you do not sufficiently consider the value of so incomparable a marvel as this horse has proved itself to be, or how great would be my chagrin if any other monarch came to possess it. And though I have not yet agreed to the Indian's proposal, I cannot incontinently reject it. But first I must be satisfied that the horse will obey other hands besides those of its inventor, else, though I become its possessor, I may find it useless."

The Indian, who had stood aside during this discussion, was now full of hope, for he perceived that the King had not altogether rejected his terms, and nothing seemed likelier than that the more he became familiar with the properties of the magic horse the more would he wish to possess it. When, therefore, the King proposed that the horse should be put to a more independent trial under another rider, the Indian readily agreed; the more so when the prince himself, relinquishing his apparent opposition, came forward and volunteered for the essay.

The King having consented, the prince mounted, and eager in his design to give his father opportunity for cooler reflection, he did not wait to hear all the Indian's instructions, but turning the peg, as he had seen the other do when first mounting, caused the horse to rise suddenly in the air, and was carried away out of sight in an easterly direction more swiftly than an arrow shot from a bow.

No sooner had the horse and its rider disappeared than the King became greatly concerned for his son's safety; and though the sage could justly excuse himself on the ground that the young prince's impatience had caused him to cut short the instructions which would have insured his safe return, the King choose to vent upon the Indian the full weight of his displeasure; and cursing the day wherein he had first set eyes on the magic horse, he caused its maker to be thrown into prison, declaring that if the prince did not return within a stated time the life of the other should be forfeit.

The Indian had now good cause to repent of the ambition which had brought him to this extremity, for the prince, of whose opposition to his project he had been thoroughly informed, had only to prolong his absence to involve him in irretrievable ruin. But on the failure of arrogant pretensions the sympathy of the judicious is wasted; let us return therefore to Prince Firouz Schah, whom we left flying through the air with incredible swiftness on the back of the magic steed.

As he descended, the daylight in which hitherto he had been travelling faded from view.

For a time, confident of his skill as a rider and undismayed either by the speed or altitude of his flight, the prince had no wish to return to the palace; but presently the thought of his father's anxiety occurred to him, and being of a tender and considerate disposition he immediately endeavoured to divert his steed from its forward course. This he sought to do by turning in the contrary direction the peg which he had handled when mounting, but to his astonishment the horse responded by rising still higher in the air and flying forward with redoubled swiftness. Had courage then deserted him, his situation might have become perilous; but preserving his accustomed coolness he began carefully to search for the means by which the speed of the machine might be abated, and before long he perceived under the horse's mane a smaller peg, which he had no sooner touched than he felt himself descending rapidly toward the earth, with a speed that lessened the nearer he came to ground.

As he descended, the daylight in which hitherto he had been travelling faded from view, and he passed within a few minutes from sunset into an obscurity so dense that he could no longer distinguish the nature of his environment, till, as the horse alighted, he perceived beneath him a smooth expanse ending abruptly on all sides at an apparent elevation among the objects surrounding it.

Dismounting he found himself on the roof of a large palace, with marble balustrades dividing it in terraces, and at one side a staircase which led down to the interior. With a spirit ever ready for adventure Prince Firouz Schah immediately descended, groping his way through the darkness till he came to a landing on the further side of which an open door led into a room where a dim light was burning.

The prince paused at the doorway to listen, but all he could hear was the sound of men breathing heavily in their sleep. He pushed the door and entered; and there across an inner threshold he saw black eunuchs lying asleep, each with a drawn sword in his hand. Immediately he guessed that something far more fair must lie beyond; so, undeterred by the danger, he advanced, and stepping lightly across their swords passed through silken hangings into the inner chamber. Here he perceived, amid surroundings of regal magnificence, a number of couches, one of which stood higher than the rest. Upon each of these a fair damsel lay asleep; but upon that which was raised above its fellows lay a form of such perfect and enchanting beauty that the prince had no will or power to turn away after once beholding it. Approaching the sleeper softly, he kneeled down and plucked her gently by the sleeve; and immediately the princess—for such if rank and beauty accorded she needs must be—opened to him the depths of her lustrous eyes and gazed in quiet amazement at the princely youth whose handsome looks and reverent demeanour banished at once all thought of alarm.

He saw black eunuchs lying asleep.

Now it so happened that a son of the King of India was at that time seeking the hand of the princess in marriage; but her father, the King of Bengal, had rejected him owing to his ferocious and disagreeable aspect. When therefore the princess saw one of royal appearance kneeling before her she supposed he could be no other than the suitor whom she knew only by report, and shedding upon him the light of her regard, "By Allah," she said, smiling, "my father lied in saying that good looks were lacking to thee!"

Prince Firouz Schah, perceiving from these words and the glance which accompanied them, that her disposition towards him was favourable, no longer feared to acquaint her with the plight in which he found himself; while the princess, for her part, listened to the story of his adventures with lively interest, and learned, not without secret satisfaction, that her visitor possessed a rank and dignity equal to her own.

She gave orders for a rich banquet to be prepared.

Meanwhile the maidens who were in attendance on the princess had awakened in dismay to the unaccountable apparition of a fair youth kneeling at the feet of their mistress, and, dreading discovery by the attendants, were all at a loss what to do. The princess however, seeing that they were awake, called them to her with perfect composure and bade them go instantly and prepare an inner chamber where the prince might sleep and recover from the fatigues of his journey; at the same time she gave orders for a rich banquet to be prepared against the time when he should be ready to partake of it. Then when her visitor had retired, she arose and began to adorn herself in jewels and rich robes and to anoint her body with fragrance, giving her women no rest till the tale of her mirror contented her; and when all had been done many times over, and the last touch of art added to her loveliness, she sent to inquire whether the prince had yet awaked and were ready to receive her.

Till the tale of her mirror contented her.

Upon the receipt of that message the prince rose eagerly, and dressing in haste, although it was scarcely yet day, heard everywhere within the palace sounds of preparation for the feast that was being got ready in his honour.

Before long the princess herself entered to inquire how he had slept, and being fully assured on that score, she gave orders for the banquet to be served. Everything was done in the greatest magnificence, but the princess was full of apologies, declaring the entertainment unworthy of so distinguished a guest. "You must pardon me, prince," she said, "for receiving you with so little state, and after so hasty a preparation; but the chief of the eunuchs does not enter here without my express permission, and I feared that elsewhere our conversation might be interrupted."

She cried: "O miserable man what sorry watch is this that thou hast kept".

Prince Firouz Schah was now convinced that the inclinations of the princess corresponded with his own; but though her every word and movement increased the tenderness of his passion, he did not forget the respect due to her rank and virtue. One of her women attendants however, seeing clearly in what direction matters were tending, and fearing for herself the results of a sudden discovery, withdrew secretly, saying nothing to the rest, and running quickly to the chief of the eunuchs she cried, "O miserable man, what sorry watch is this that thou hast kept, guarding the King's honour; and who is this man or genie that thou hast admitted to the presence of our mistress? Nay, if the matter be not already past remedy the fault is not thine!" At these words the eunuch leapt up in alarm, and going secretly he lifted the curtain of the inner chamber, and there beheld at the princess's side a youth of such fair and majestical appearance that he durst not intrude unbidden. He ran shrieking to the King, and as he went he rent his garments and threw dust upon his head. "O sire and master," he cried, "come quickly and save thy daughter, for there is with her a genie in mortal form and like a king's son to look upon, and if he have not already carried her away, make haste and give orders that he be seized, lest thou become childless."

The King at once arose and went in great haste and fear to his daughters palace. There he was met by certain of her women, who, seeing his alarm, said, "O sire, have no fear for the safety of thy daughter; for this young man is as handsome of heart as of person, and as his conduct is chaste, so also are his intentions honourable."

Then the King's wrath was cooled somewhat; but since much remained which demanded explanation he drew his sword and advanced with a threatening aspect into the room where his daughter and the prince still sat conversing. Prince Firouz Schah observing the new-comer advance upon him in a warlike attitude, drew his own sword and stood ready for defence; whereupon the King, seeing that the other was the stronger, sheathed his weapon, and with a gesture of salutation addressed him courteously. "Tell me, fair youth," he said, "whether you are man or devil, for though in appearance you are human, how else than by devilry have you come here?"

"Sire," replied the youth, "but for the respect that is owing to the father of so fair a daughter, I, whom am a son of kings, might resent such an imputation. Be assured, however, that by whatever means I have chosen to arrive, my intentions now are altogether human and honourable; for I have no other or dearer wish than to become your son-in-law through my marriage with this princess in whose eyes it is my happiness to have found favour."

"What you tell me," answered the King, "may be all very true; but it is not the custom for the sons of kings to enter into palaces without the permission of their owners, coming, moreover, unannounced and with no retinue or mark of royalty about them. How, then, shall I convince my people that you are a fit suitor for the hand of my daughter?"

"The proof of honour and kingship," answered the other, "does not rest in splendour and retinue alone, though these also would be at my call had I the patience to await their arrival from that too distant country where my father is king. Let it suffice if I shall be able to prove my worth alone and unaided, in such a manner as to satisfy all." "Alone and unaided?" said the King; "how may that be?" "I will prove it thus," answered the prince. "Call out your troops and let them surround this palace; tell them that you have here a stranger, of whom nothing is known, who declares that if you will not yield him the hand of your daughter in marriage he will carry her away from you by force. Bid them use all means to capture and slay me, and if I survive so unequal a contest, judge then whether or no I am fit to become your son-in-law."

The King immediately accepted the proposal, agreeing to abide by the result; yet was he grieved that a youth of such fair looks and promise should throw away his life in so foolhardy an adventure. As soon as day dawned he sent for his Vizier and bade him cause all the chiefs of his army to assemble with their troops and companies, till presently there were gathered about the palace forty thousand horsemen and the same number of foot; and the King gave them instructions, saying, "When the young man of whom I have warned you comes forth and challenges you to battle, then fall upon and slay him, for in no wise must he escape." He then led the prince to an open space whence he could see the whole army drawn up in array against him. "Yonder," said the King, pointing, "are those with whom you have to contend; go forth and deal with them as seems best to you."

"Nay," answered the prince, "these are not fair conditions, for yonder I see horsemen as well as foot; how shall I contend against these unless I be mounted?" The King at once offered him the best horse in his stables, but the prince would not hear of it. "Is it fair," he said, "that I should trust my life under such conditions to a horse that I have never ridden? I will ride no horse but that upon which I came hither." "Where is that?" inquired the King. "If it be where I left it," answered the prince, "it is upon the roof of the palace."

All who heard this answer were filled with laughter and astonishment, for it seemed impossible that a horse could have climbed to so high a roof. Nevertheless the King commanded that search should be made, and there, sure enough, those that were sent found the horse of ebony and ivory standing stiff and motionless. So though it still seemed to them but a thing for jest and mockery, obeying the King's orders they raised it upon their shoulders, and bearing it to earth carried it forth into the open space before the palace where the King's troops were assembled.

Then Prince Firouz Schah advanced, and leaping upon the horse he cried defiance to the eighty thousand men that stood in battle array against him. And they, on their part, seeing the youth so hardily set on his own destruction, drew sword and couched spear, and came all together to the charge. The prince waited till they were almost upon him, then turning the peg which stood in the pommel of his saddle he caused the horse to rise suddenly in the air, and all the foremost ranks of the enemy came clashing together beneath him. At that sight the King and all his court drew a breath of astonishment, and the army staggered and swung about this way and that, striking vainly up at the hoofs of the magic horse as it flew over them. Then the King, full of dread lest this should indeed be some evil genie that sought to carry his daughter away from him, called to his archers to shoot, but before they could make ready their bows Prince Firouz Schah had given another turn to the peg, and immediately the horse sprang upward and rose higher than the roof of the palace, so that all the arrows fell short and rained destruction on those that were below.

Then the prince called to the King, "O King of Bengal, have I not now proved myself worthy to be thy son-in-law, and wilt thou not give me the hand of thy daughter in marriage?" But the King's wrath was very great, for he had been made foolish in the eyes of his people, and panic had broken the ranks of his army and many of them were slain; and by no means would he have for his son-in-law one that possessed such power to throw down the order and establishment of his kingdom. So he cried back to the prince, saying, "O vile enchanter, get hence as thou valuest thy life, for if ever thou darest to return and set foot within my dominions thy death and not my daughter shall be thy reward!" Thus he spoke in his anger, forgetting altogether the promise he had made.

Now it should be known that all this time the princess had been watching the combat from the roof of the palace; and as her fear and anxiety for the prince had in the first instance been great, so now was she overjoyed when she saw him rise superior to the dangers which had threatened him. But as soon as she heard her father's words she became filled with fresh fear lest she and her lover were now to be parted; so as the prince came speeding by upon the magic horse she stretched up her arms to him, crying, "O master of the flying bird, leave me not desolate, for if thou goest from me now I shall die."

All this time the Princess had been watching the combat from the roof of the palace.

No sooner did Prince Firouz Schah hear those words than he checked his steed in its flight, and swooping low he bore down over the palace roof, and catching the princess up in his arms placed her upon the saddle before him; and straightway at the pressure of its rider the horse rose under them and carried them away high in air, so that they disappeared forthwith from the eyes of the King and his people.

But as they travelled the day grew hot and the sun burned fiercely upon them; and the prince looking down beheld a green meadow by the side of a lake; so he said, "O desire of my heart, let us go down into yonder meadow and seek rest and refreshment, and there let us wait till it is evening, so that we may come unperceived to my fathers palace; and when I have brought thee thither safely and secretly, then will I make preparation so that thou mayest appear at my fathers court in such a manner as befits thy rank."

In the garden of the summer palace all was silence and solitude.

So the princess consenting, they went down and sat by the lake and solaced themselves sweetly with love till it was evening. Then they rose up and mounted once more upon the magic horse and came by night to the outskirts of the city where dwelt the King of Persia. Now in the garden of the summer palace which stood without the walls all was silence and solitude, and coming thither unperceived the King's son led the princess to a pavilion, the door of which lay open, and placing before it the magic horse he bade her stay within and keep watch till his messenger should come to take her to the palace which he would cause to be prepared for her.

Sat by the lake and solaced themselves sweetly with love.

Leaving her thus safely sheltered, the prince went in to the city to present himself before the King his father; and there he found him in deep mourning and affliction because of his son's absence; and his father seeing him, rose up and embraced him tenderly, rejoicing because of his safe return, and eager to know in what way he had fared. And the prince said, "O my father, if it be thy good will and pleasure, I have come back to thee far richer than I went. For I have brought with me the fairest princess that the eyes of love have ever looked upon, and she is the daughter of the King of Bengal; and because of my love for her and the great service which she rendered me when I was a stranger in the midst of enemies, therefore have I no heart or mind or will but to win your consent that I may marry her." And when the King heard that, and of all that the princess had done, and of how they had escaped together, he gave his consent willingly, and ordered that a palace should be immediately got ready for her reception that she might on the next day appear before the people in a manner befitting her rank.

Then while preparation was going forward, the prince sought news concerning the sage, for he feared that the King might have slain him. "Do not speak of him," cried the King. "Would to Heaven that I had never set eyes on him or his invention, for out of this has arisen all my grief and lamentation. Therefore he now lies in prison awaiting death."

"Nay," said the prince "now surely should he be released and suitably rewarded, seeing that unwittingly he hath been the cause of my fortune; but do not give him my sister in marriage."

So the King sent and caused the Indian to be brought before him clad in a robe of rank. And the King said to him, "Because my son, whom thy vile invention carried away from me, hath returned safe and sound, therefore will I spare thy life. And for the reward of thine ingenuity I give thee this robe of honour; but now take thy horse, wherever it may be, and go, nor ever appear in my sight again. And if thou wilt marry, seek one of thine own rank, but do not aspire to the daughters of kings."

When the Indian heard that, he dissembled his rage, and bowing himself to the earth departed from the King's presence. And, as he went, everywhere in the palace ran the tale how the King's son had returned upon the magic horse, bringing with him a princess of most marvellous beauty, and how they had alighted in the gardens of the summer palace that lay outside the walls.

Now when this was told him the Indian at once saw his opportunity, and going forth from the city in haste he arrived at the summer palace before the messenger with the appointed retinue which the prince and the King were sending. So coming to the pavilion in the garden he found the princess waiting within, and before the door the horse of ivory and ebony. Then was his heart uplifted for joy, the more so when he perceived how far the damsel exceeded in loveliness all that had been told of her. Entering the chamber where she sat he kissed the ground at her feet; and she, seeing one that wore a robe of office making obeisance before her, speak to him without fear, saying, "Who art thou?"

The sage answered, "O moon of beauty, I am but the dust which lies upon the road by which thou art to travel. Yet I come as a messenger from the King's son who hath sent me to bring thee with all speed to a chamber in the royal palace where he now awaits thee."

Now the Indian was of a form altogether hideous and abominable. The princess looked at him, therefore, in surprise, saying, "Could not the King's son find any one to send to me but thee?" The sage laughed, for he read the meaning of her words. "O searcher of hearts," he said, "do not wonder that the prince hath sent to thee a man whose looks are unattractive, for because of his love toward thee he is grown exceeding jealous. Were it otherwise, I doubt not that he would have chosen the highest and most honourable in the land; but, being what I am, he has preferred to make me his messenger."

When the princess heard that, she believed him, and because her impatience to be with her lover was great, she yielded herself willingly into his hands. Then the sage mounted upon the horse and took up the damsel behind him; and having bound her to his girdle for safety, he turned the pin so swiftly that immediately they rose up into the air far above the roof of the palace and in full view of the royal retinue which was even then approaching.

Now because his desire to be with his beloved was so strong, the prince himself had come forth before all others to meet her; and when he saw her thus carried away captive, he uttered a loud cry of lamentation, and stretched out his hands toward her. The cry of her lover reached the ears of the princess, and looking down she saw with wonder his gestures of grief and despair. So she said to the Indian, "O slave, why art thou bearing me away from thy lord, disobeying his command?" The sage answered, "He is not my lord, nor do I owe him any duty or obedience.

May Heaven repay on him all the grief he has brought on me, for I was the maker of this horse on which he won thee, and because he stole it from me I was cast into prison. But now for all my wrongs I will take full payment, and will torture his heart as he hath tortured mine. Be of good cheer, therefore, for doubt not that presently I shall seem a more desirable lover in thine eyes than ever he was."

On hearing these words the princess was so filled with terror and loathing that she endeavoured to cast herself from the saddle; but the Indian having bound her to his girdle, no present escape from him was possible.

The horse had meanwhile carried them far from the city of the King of Persia, and it was yet an early hour after dawn when they arrived over the land of Cashmire. Assured that he was now safe from pursuit, and perceiving an uninhabited country below him, the Indian caused the horse to descend on the edge of a wood bordered by a stream. Here he made the princess dismount, and was proceeding to force upon her his base and familiar attentions, when the cries raised by the princess drew to that spot a party of horsemen who had been hunting in the neighbourhood. The leader of the party, who chanced to be no other than the Sultan of that country, seeing a fair damsel undergoing ill-treatment from one of brutish and malevolent aspect, rode forward and demanded of the Indian by what right he so used her. The sage boldly declared that she was his wife and that how he used her was no man's business but his own. The damsel, however, contradicted his assertion with indignation and scorn, and so great were her beauty and the dignity of her bearing that her statement of the case had only to be heard to be believed. The Sultan therefore ordered the Indian to be bound and beaten, and afterwards to be led away to the adjacent city and there cast into the deepest dungeon. As for the princess and magic horse, he caused them to be brought to the palace; and there for the damsel he provided a magnificent apartment with slaves and attendants such as befitted her rank; but the horse, whose properties remained secret, since no other use for it could be discovered, was placed in the royal treasury.

Now though the princess was full of joy over her escape from the Indian, and of gratitude to her deliverer, she could not fail to read in the Sultan's manner towards her the spell cast by her beauty. And, in fact, no later than the next day, awakened by sounds throughout the whole city of tumult and rejoicing, and inquiring as to the reason, she was informed that these festivities were the prelude to her own nuptials with the Sultan which were to be celebrated that very day before sundown.

At this news her consternation was so great that she immediately swooned away, and remained for a long while speechless. But no sooner had she recovered possession of her faculties than her resolution was formed, and when the Sultan entered, as is customary on such occasions, to present his compliments and make inquiries as to her health, she fell into an extravagance of attitude and speech, so artfully contrived that all who beheld her became convinced of her insanity. And the more surely to effect her purpose, and at the same time to relieve her feelings, she made a violent attack upon the Sultan's person; nor did she desist until she had brought him to recognize that all hopes for the present consummation of the nuptials were useless.

On the following day also, and upon every succeeding one, the princess showed the same violent symptoms whenever the Sultan approached her. It was in vain that all the wisest physicians in the country were summoned into consultation. While some declared that her malady was curable, others, to whose word the princess by her actions lent every possible weight, declared that it was incurable; and in no case was any remedy applied that did not seem immediately to aggravate the disorder.

It was in vain that all the wisest physicians in the country were summoned into consultation.

And here for a while we must leave the princess and return to Prince Firouz Schah, whose affliction no words can describe. Unable to endure the burden of his beloved one's absence in the splendours of his father's palace, or to leave her the victim of fate without an attempt at rescue, he put on the disguise of a travelling dervish, and departing secretly from the Persian court set out into the world to seek for her.

For many months he travelled without clue or tidings to guide him; but as Heaven ever bestows favour on constancy in love, so it led him at last to the land of Cashmire, and to the city of its Sultan. Now as he drew near to it by the main road, he fell into conversation with a certain merchant, and inquired of him as to the city and the life and conditions of its inhabitants. And the merchant looked at him in surprise, saying, "Surely you have come from a far country not to have heard of the strange things which have happened here, for everywhere in these regions and among all the caravans goes the story of the strange maiden, and the ebony horse, and the waiting nuptials."

For many months he travelled without clue.

Now when the prince heard that, he knew that the end of his wanderings was in sight: so looking upon the city with eyes of gladness, "Tell me," he said, "for I know none of these things." So the merchant told him truly all that has here been narrated; and having ended he said, "O dervish, though you are young, you have in your eyes the light of wisdom; and if you have also in your hands the power of healing, then I tell you that in this city fortune awaits you, for the Sultan will give even the half of his kingdom to any man that shall restore health of mind to this damsel."

Then the King's son felt his heart uplifted within him, howbeit he knew well that the fortune he sought would not be of the Sultan's choosing; so parting from the merchant, he put on the robe of a physician, and went and presented himself at the palace.

And ever with the tears falling down from her eyes she sighed and sang.

The Sultan was glad at his coming, for though many physicians had promised healing and had all failed, still each new arrival gave him fresh hopes. Now as the sight of a physician seemed ever greatly to increase the princess's malady, the Sultan led him to a small closet or balcony, that thence he might look upon her unperceived. So Prince Firouz Schah, having travelled so many miles in search of her, saw his beloved seated in deep despondency by the side of a fountain; and ever with the tears falling down from her eyes she sighed and sang. Now when he heard her voice and the words, and beheld the soft grief of her countenance, then the prince knew that her disorder was only feigned; and he went forth and said to the Sultan, "This malady is curable; but for the cure something is yet lacking. Let me go in and speak with the damsel alone, and on my life I promise that if all be done according to my requirements, before this time to-morrow the cure shall be accomplished."

At these words the Sultan rejoiced greatly, and he ordered the doors of the princess's chamber to be opened to the physician. So Firouz Schah passed in, and he and his beloved were alone together. Now because of his grief and wanderings and the growth of his beard, the face of the prince was so changed that the princess did not know him; but seeing one before her in the dress of a physician she rose up in pretended frenzy and began to throw herself about with violence, until from utter exhaustion she fell prostrate. Thereupon the prince drew near, and called her gently by name; and immediately when she heard his voice she knew him, and uttered a loud cry. Then the king's son put his mouth to her ear and said "O temptation of all hearts, now spare my life and have patience, for surely I am come to save thee; but if the Sultan learn who I am we are dead, thou and I, because his jealousy is great." So she replied, saying, "O thou that bringest me life, tell me what I shall do?" The prince said, "When I depart hence let it appear that I have restored to thee the possession of thy faculties; howbeit the full cure is to come after. Therefore when the Sultan comes to thee, be sad and meek and do not repulse him as thou hast done aforetime. Yet have no fear but that I will keep thee safe from him to the last." And so saying he left the princess and returned to the Sultan, and said to him, "Go in and see whether the cure be not already at work; but approach not near to her, for though the genie that possessed her is bound he is not yet cast forth: nevertheless to-morrow before noon the remedy shall be complete."

So the Sultan went and found her even as he had been told; and with joy and gratitude he returned to Firouz Schah, saying, "Truly thou art a healer and the rest are but bunglers and fools. Now, therefore, give orders and all shall be done according to thy will. Doubt not that thy reward shall be great."

Then the prince said, "Let the horse of ivory and ebony which was with her at the first be brought forth and set again in the place where it was found, and let the damsel also be brought and put into my hand; and it shall be that when I have set her upon the horse, then the evil genie that held her shall be suddenly loosed, passing from her into that which was aforetime his place of bondage. So shall the remedy be complete, and the princess find joy in her lord before the eyes of all."

Now when the Sultan heard that, the mystery of the ebony horse seemed plain to him, and its use manifest. Therefore he gave orders that with all speed the thing should be done as the physician of the princess required it.

So early on the morrow they brought the horse from the royal treasury, and the princess from her chamber, and carried them to the place where they were first found; and all about, a great crowd of the populace was gathered to behold the sight. Then Prince Firouz Schah took the princess and set her upon the horse, and leaping into the saddle before her he turned the pin of ascent, and immediately the horse rose with a great sound into the air, and hung above the heads of the affrighted populace. And the King's son leaned down from the saddle and cried in a loud voice, "O Sultan of Cashmire, when you wish to espouse princesses which seek your protection, learn first to obtain their consent." And so saying he put the horse to its topmost speed, and like an arrow on the wind he and the princess were borne away, and passed and vanished, and were no more seen in that land.

But in the city of the King of Persia great joy and welcome and thanksgiving awaited them; and there without delay the nuptials were solemnized and through all the country the people rejoiced and feasted for a full month. But because of the grief and affliction that it had caused him the King broke the ebony horse and destroyed its motions. As for the maker thereof, the Sultan of Cashmire caused him to be put to a cruel death: and thus is the story of the sage and his invention brought to a full ending.

THE STORY OF THE WICKED HALF-BROTHERS

In the city of Harran there once lived a King who had every happiness which life and fortune could bestow save that he lacked an heir. Although, according to royal custom, he had in his household fifty wives, fair to look upon and affectionate in disposition, and though he continually invoked on these unions the blessing of Heaven, still he remained childless; for which cause all his joy was turned to affliction, and his wealth and power and magnificence became as of no account.

There appeared before him an old man of venerable appearance.

Now one night as he slept there appeared before him an old man of venerable appearance who, addressing him in mild accents, spoke thus: "The prayer of the faithful among fifty has been heard. Arise, therefore and, go into the gardens of your palace and cause the gardener to bring you a pomegranate fully ripe. Eat as many of the seeds as you desire children, and your wish shall be fulfilled."

Pirouzè, the fairest and most honourably born.

Immediately upon awaking the King remembered the dream, and going down into the gardens of the palace he took fifty pomegranate seeds, and counting them one by one ate them all. So in due course according to the promise of his dream, each of his wives gave birth to a son all about the same time. To this, however, there was an exception, for one of the fifty whose name was Pirouzè, the fairest and the most honourably born, she alone, as time went on, showed no sign of that which was expected of her. Then was the King's anger kindled against her because in her alone the promise of his dream was not fulfilled; and deeming such a one hateful in the eyes of Heaven he was minded to put her to death. His vizier, however, dissuaded him. "Time alone can show," said he, "whether her demerits are so great as you now suppose. Let her go back to her own people and remain in banishment until the will of Heaven shall declare itself, and if within due time she give birth to a son then can she return to you with all honour." So the King did as his vizier advised, and sent Pirouzè back to her own country to the court of the Prince of Samaria; and there before long she who had seemed barren had the joy of becoming a mother and gave birth to a son whom she named Codadad, that is to say, "the Gift of God." Nevertheless, because the King of Harran had put upon her so public a disgrace, the Prince of Samaria would send no word to him of the event; so the young Prince was brought up at his uncle's court, and there he learned to ride and to shoot and to perform such warlike feats as become a prince, and in all that country he had no equal for accomplishment or courage.

Now one day, when Codadad had reached the age of eighteen, word came to him that his father the King of Harran was engaged in war and surrounded by enemies; so the Prince said to his mother, "Now is it time that I should go and prove myself worthy of my birth and the equal of my brethren; for here in Samaria all is peace and indolence, but in Harran are hardship and dangers, and great deeds waiting to be done." And his mother said to him, "O my son, since it seems good to thee, go; but how wilt thou declare thyself to thy father, or cause him to believe thy word, seeing that he is ignorant of thy birth?" Codadad answered, "I will so declare myself by my deeds that before my father knows the truth he shall wish that it were true."

So he departed and came in princely arms to the city of Harran, and there offered his service to the King against all his enemies. Now, no sooner had the King looked upon the youth than his heart was drawn toward him because of his beauty and the secret ties of blood, but when he asked from what country he came, Codadad answered, "I am the son of an emir of Cairo, and wherever there is war I go to win fame, nor do I care in what cause I fight so long as I be proved worthy."

The Prince was not slow in making his valour known; before long he had risen to the command of the whole army, not only over the heads of his brethren but also of the more experienced officers. And thereafter, when peace was re-established, the King, finding Codadad as prudent as he was valiant, appointed him governor to the young Princes.

Now this act, though justified by merit, could not fail to increase the hatred and jealousy which Codadad's brethren had long felt towards him. "What?" they cried, "shall this stranger not only steal from us the first place in the King's favour, but must we also be in obedience to his ruling and judgment? Surely if we do so we are no sons of a King."

So they conspired together how best to be rid of him. One said, "Let us fall upon him with our swords." "No, no," said another, "for so doing we shall but bring punishment upon ourselves. But let us so arrange matters as to draw on him the weight of the King's anger; thus shall our vengeance be made both safe and complete."

To this the other Princes agreed; so forming a design which seemed favourable to their end they approached Codadad, and besought his permission to go forth together on a hunting expedition, promising to return the same day. Codadad, deeming the request reasonable, immediately granted it: the brothers departed, but they did not return.

On the third day the King made inquiry as to the reason of their absence. Codadad replied that they were gone on a hunting expedition but had promised to return much sooner. Another day passed and the King grew anxious; yet another, and he became furious; and all his wrath was directed against Codadad. "O traitor," he cried, "why has thou neglected thy trust and allowed my sons to go anywhere unaccompanied by thee? Now go instantly and search for them, and if thou find them not be assured that on thy head shall fall the penalty."

At these words the Prince was filled with sudden foreboding, for he knew that the brothers had no love for him, and well could he see now the danger into which he had fallen. All he could do, however, was to obey; so furnishing himself with arms and a horse good for travelling, he set out in search of his brethren.

After some days employed in a fruitless quest he came to a desolate tract in the midst of which stood a castle of black marble. As he approached he beheld at an upper window a damsel of marvellous beauty, with torn garments, dishevelled hair, and a countenance expressive of the most lively affliction, who immediately that she set eyes on him wrung her hands and waived him away crying "Oh, fly, fly from this place of death and the monster which inhabits it! For here lives a black giant which feeds on human flesh, seizing all he can find. Even now in his dungeons you may hear the cries of those whom for his next meal he will devour."

"Madam," replied the Prince, "for my safety you need have no care. Only be good enough to inform me who you are and how you came to be in your present plight." "I come from Cairo," she replied, "where my birth gives me rank. And as I was travelling from thence on my road to Bagdad this monstrous negro suddenly fell upon us, and having slain my escort brought me hither a captive, to endure, if Heaven refuses me succour, things far worse than death. But though I know my own peril I will not see others perish in a vain attempt to rescue me, therefore once more I entreat you to fly ere it be too late!"

Reaching his farthest wounded the giant in the knee.

But even as she spoke, the negro, a horrible and gigantic monster of loathsome appearance, came in sight moving rapidly toward the palace. No sooner had he caught sight of the Prince than he rushed upon him with growls of fury, and drawing his scimitar aimed at him a blow which, had it found him, must there and then have ended the fight. The Prince, however, swerved nimbly under the stroke, and reaching his farthest, wounded the giant in the knee; then wheeling his charger about before the negro could turn on his maimed limb he attacked him from the rear, and with one fortunate blow brought him to earth. Instantly, before the giant could gather up his huge length and regain his vantage, Codadad spurred forward and with a single sweep of his sword smote off his head.

Meanwhile, all breathless above, the lady had leaned watching the contest. Now, seeing that victory was secured, she gave free vent to her joy and gratitude. "O prince of men!" she cried, "now is revealed to me the high rank to which thou wast born. Finish, then, thy work; take from the girdle of yonder wretch the keys of the castle and come quickly to the release of me and my fellow prisoners."

The lady advanced to meet him.

The Prince did according to her directions; as he opened the gates and entered the forecourt the lady advanced to meet him, ready, had he permitted it, to throw herself in gratitude at his feet. And now, as he beheld near at hand the beauty which had charmed him from a distance, Codadad realized how great had been his fortune, and with his whole heart rejoiced at the deliverance of one in whose nature so much virtue and grace seemed blended.

But while he was thus lost in the contemplation of her loveliness there arose from the basement of the castle a dreadful sound of crying and lamentation. "What is that?" inquired the Prince. "It is the cry of the prisoners," replied the lady, "to whom, I doubt not, the opening of the gates has betokened the monster's return. Come, therefore, quickly and relieve them of their misery." And so saying she pointed to the door which led to the place of confinement.

Thither, accompanied by the lady, went Codadad with all speed. Descending by a dark stair he came upon a vast cavern dimly lighted, around the walls of which a hundred prisoners lay chained. Instantly he set to work to loose their bonds, informing them at the same time of the death of their captor and of their freedom from all further danger. At these unexpected tidings the captives raised a cry of joy and thanksgiving; but great as was their surprise at such unlooked-for deliverance, greater still was that of the Prince when, on bringing them to the light, he discovered that forty-nine of the hundred whom he had released were his own brethren.

The Princes received the cordial embraces of their deliverer with little embarrassment, for the disaster into which they had fallen had caused them almost entirely to forget their original intent. Satisfied with expressing in proper terms their obligation and gratitude toward Codadad, they now joined eagerly in his survey of the castle; there upon examination they found an extraordinary variety and wealth of booty, consisting for the most part of merchandise which the negro had pillaged from passing caravans, some of it actually belonging to those whom Codadad had so recently rescued.

The Prince accordingly ordered the merchants each to take what he recognized as his own; and this being done he divided the rest equally between them. The question then arose how they should remove their plunder from a place so desolately situated, where it would seem impossible to procure means of conveyance; but on a further search they found not only the camels of the merchants, but also the horses on which the Princes of Harran had ridden; and as, at their approach the black slaves who were in charge of the stables fell into headlong flight, Codadad and his companions found themselves left in undisputed possession. The merchants therefore loaded their camels, and with renewed protestations of gratitude departed on the several roads by which their avocations called them.

When they were gone Codadad's next care was to inquire of the lady in what direction she wished to travel, promising that he and the Princes would conduct her in safety to any place she might name. The lady replied, thanking him for his generous offer. "But wherever I go," said she, "it cannot be to my own country, for not only is it too far distant, but cruel misfortune has separated me from it for ever. And since you have put me under so great an obligation, let me now confess the truth which before I thought it prudent to conceal. My dignity of rank is far higher than that to which I recently laid claim; in me you behold a King's daughter, and if it will interest you to hear the story of my misfortunes, I shall be happy to recount it." Assured of the lively sympathy of her auditors she began as follows:

THE STORY OF THE PRINCESS OF DERYABAR

A city among the Isles named Deryabar.

My father was the King of a city among the isles named Deryabar, and I was his only child; for, in spite of his many prayers directed to that end, Heaven had not granted him a son. And for this cause, though he bestowed upon my education all imaginable care, the sight of me remained displeasing to him. In order the better to forget his sorrow he spent his days in hunting, and so he chanced on the event which led to all our misfortunes. For one day, as he was riding unattended in the forest, night overtook him and he knew not which way to turn. Presently in the distance he perceived a light, and advancing towards it he came upon a hut within which a monstrous negro stood basting an ox that roasted before the fire. In the further corner of the hut lay a beautiful woman with hands bound, and a face betokening the deepest affliction, while at her feet a young child, between two and three years of age, stretched up its arms and wailed without ceasing.

Presently in the distance he perceived a light.

At this sight my father was filled with compassion, but his desire to effect her rescue was restrained for a while by fear that a failure might only make matters worse. In the meantime the giant, having drained a pitcher of wine, sat down to eat. Presently he turned himself about and addressed the lady. "Charming Princess," said he, "why will you not accept the good things which are within your reach? Only yield to me the love that I demand and you will find in me the gentlest and most considerate of lords." To these advances, however, the lady replied with resolution and courage. "Vile monster," she cried, "every time I look at you does but increase my hatred and loathing toward you. Unchangeable as the foulness of your appearance is the disgust with which you inspire me!"

These words of violent provocation were no sooner uttered than the negro, beside himself with rage, drew his sword, and seizing the lady by the hair, lifted her from the ground in preparation for the blow that would have ended all. Whereupon, seeing that not a moment was to be lost, my father drew his bow and let fly an arrow with so good an aim that pierced to the heart the giant fell dead. Immediately entering the hut my father raised the lady from the swoon into which she had fallen, and severing her bonds gave her the needed reassurance that all danger was now over. Before long he learned in answer to his inquiries that she had been wife to a chief of the Saracens, in whose service the slain giant had, on account of his great strength, occupied a position of trust. This, however, he had shamelessly betrayed; for having conceived a violent passion for his master's wife, he first persuaded the chief into an expedition which terminated in his death, and then returning in haste carried away by force not only the lady but her child also. From this degrading bondage my father's act had now saved her; but though thus relieved of immediate danger, the wife of the Saracen chief was both solitary and friendless, for not only was she too far removed from her own land to return to it unaided, but she had small hope, should she ever arrive there, of securing for her son his rightful inheritance. This being the case my father, moved with compassion, determined to adopt the child as his own; and as the lady gratefully accepted his proposal, the next day as soon as it was light he returned to Deryabar bringing with him mother and son.

Thus it came about that the son of a Saracen chief was brought up in my father's palace like a Prince of the blood royal; and so, on attaining to manhood, having both grace and good looks to recommend him, he came to forget the comparative lowliness of his origin, and aspiring to become my father's heir, had the presumption to demand my hand in marriage.

A claim so audacious merited the severest punishment, yet my father merely remarked that he had other views concerning me, and with so lenient a rebuke would have passed the matter by. His refusal, however, excited in the proud youth the liveliest resentment; seeing that he could not obtain his ambition by fair means he immediately entered into conspiracy, and having treacherously slain my father, caused himself to be made King in his place. Fresh from this monstrous crime he renewed his suit for my hand, and was preparing to enforce it by violence, when the vizier, who alone of all my fathers court had remained faithful to his memory, found means to convey me from the palace to a sailing vessel which was leaving harbour the same night.

The ship struck upon a rock.

Here for a time I seemed to have reached safety, but when we had been only three days at sea a violent storm arose, and the ship, driving helplessly before it, struck upon a rock and went down leaving as sole survivor the one who least wished to be spared. How I was saved I know not, nor how long I lay unfriended by the desolate shore upon which I had been cast; but scarcely had the consciousness of life returned to me when I heard a multitudinous sound of swift galloping; and presently, feeling myself lifted by men's hands, I turned and saw halting near me a troop of Arab horsemen, and at their head a youth royally arrayed and beautiful as the morning. Thus when my fortunes were at their lowest I beheld him whom Heaven had sent not only to afford me that deliverance of which I stood so much in need, but also to restore me to the rank due to my birth. For let me confess that after this young Prince had succoured me with the most tender solicitude, conducting me in all honour to his own palace and there lodging me under his mother's protection, I experienced towards him a feeling of duty and gratitude such as would have made his lightest wish my law. When therefore with an ardent and ever increasing devotion he desired me to become his bride, I could not, upon the completion of my recovery, refuse him the happiness he sought.

And presently, feeling myself lifted by men's hands.

But the festivities of our marriage were scarcely ended, when suddenly by night the city in which we dwelt was attacked by a band of travelling marauders. The attack was so unexpected and so well planned that the town was stormed and the garrison cut to pieces before any news of the event had reached the palace. Under cover of darkness we managed to escape, and fleeing to the sea shore took refuge on a small fishing boat, in which we immediately put out to sea, hoping to find in the rude winds and waves a safer shelter than our own walls had afforded us.

For two days we drifted with wind and tide, not knowing any better direction in which to turn; upon the third we perceived with relief a ship bearing down upon us, but as we watched its approach our satisfaction was soon changed to apprehension and dread, for we saw clearly that those on board were neither fishermen nor traders, but pirates. With rude shouts they boarded our small bark, and seizing my husband and myself carried us captive to their own vessel. Here the one who was their leader advanced towards me and pulled aside my veil; whereupon a great clamour instantly arose among the crew, each contending for the possession of me. The dispute upon this point grew so warm that presently they fell to fighting; and a bitter and deadly conflict was maintained till at last only a single pirate was left. This one, who now regarded himself as my owner, proceeded to inform me of what was to be my fate. "I have," he said, "a friend in Cairo who has promised me a rich reward if I can supply him with a slave, more beautiful than any of those that his harem now contains. The distinction of earning me this reward shall be yours." "But tell me," he went on, turning towards the place where my husband stood bound, "who is this youth that accompanies you? Is he a lover or a brother, or only a servant?" "Sir," said, I "he is my husband." "In that case" he replied, "out of pity we must get rid of him, for I would not afflict him needlessly with the sight of another's happiness." And so saying, he took my husband, all bound as he was, and threw him into the sea.

So great was my grief at the sight of this cruel deed, that had I not been bound myself I should undoubtedly have sought the same end to my sufferings. But for the sake of future profit the pirate took the most watchful care of me, not only so long as we were on board the ship but also when, a few days later, we came to port and there joined ourselves to a large caravan which was about to start on the road to Cairo. While thus travelling in apparent safety, we were suddenly attacked by the terrible negro who lately owned this castle. After a long and dubious conflict the pirate, and all who stood by him, were slain, while I and those of the merchants who had remained timorously looking on were seized, and brought hither as prisoners destined as it seemed for a fate far more lingering and terrible. The rest of my story, brave Prince, I need not here recount, since the shaping of it was so largely in your own hands, and since to you alone is owed the happiness of its conclusion.

The Princess of Deryabar.

When the Princess of Deryabar had thus finished the tale of her wanderings, Codadad hastened to assure her how deep was his sympathy in all her misfortunes. "But if you will allow yourself," he continued, "to be guided by me, your future life shall be one of safety and tranquillity. You have but to come as my bride, and the King of Harran will offer you an honourable welcome to his court; while, as regards myself, my whole life shall be devoted to securing for you that happiness which your grace and noble qualities prove that you deserve. And that you may not regard this proposal as too presumptuous, I have now to inform you, and also these Princes, concerning my birth and rank. For I, too, am a son of the King of Harran, born to him at the court of Samaria by his wife the Princess Pirouzè, whom he had sent unjustly into banishment."

This declaration on the part of Codadad so accorded with the inclinations of the Princess that she at once yielded her consent, and as the castle was full of provisions suitable for the occasion, preparations were made firstto solemnize the marriage, and then for all together to set forth on the return journey to Harran. As for the Princes, though they received Codadad's news with every outward protestation of joy, they were in fact more filled with apprehension and jealousy than before, for they could not but fear that his favour with the King would be greatly increased and become far more dangerous to their interests when the true facts of his birth were revealed. No sooner, therefore, had Codadad and the Princess passed to their nuptials, than his brethren entered into a conspiracy to slay him; and at the first halt upon the homeward journey, taking advantage of the lack of protection which a tent affords, they came upon their brother by night, and stabbing him in a hundred places as he lay asleep, left him for dead in the arms of his bride. They then broke up the camp and returned with all haste to the city of Harran, where, with a falsely invented tale they excused themselves to the King for their long absence.

In the meantime Codadad lay so spent by loss of blood that there remained in him no sign of life. The Princess, his wife, distraught with grief, had already given him up for dead. "O Heaven," she cried, bathing his body with her tears, "why am I thus ever condemned to bring on others disaster and death, and why for a second time have I been deprived of the one I was about to love?"

She found to her grief the place where Codadad had lain left vacant.

As thus she continued to cry in piteous lamentation, and to gaze on the senseless form lying before her, she thought that she perceived on the lips a faint motion of breath. At once her hope revived, and springing to her feet she ran instantly in the direction of the nearest village, hoping to find there a surgeon or one that had skill in the binding of wounds. Returning after a time with the aid that she had summoned she found to her grief the place where Codadad had lain left vacant, nor was there any trace or indication of the fate which had overtaken him.

Overwhelmed by this final catastrophe, and believing that some wild beast must have devoured him, she suffered herself to be led away by the surgeon, who, in pity for one so greatly afflicted, placed her under the shelter of his own roof, and lavished upon her every mark of consideration and respect. So, when she had sufficiently recovered, for her griefs to find utterance he gathered from her own lips all the circumstances of her story, her name and rank, the high and valiant deeds of the Prince her husband, and the base ingratitude of his brethren. And perceiving that her grief and sufferings had so robbed her of the desire of life that without some end on which to direct her will she would presently pass into a decline, the surgeon endeavoured to arouse her to the pursuit of that just vengeance which the murder of her husband had earned. "Do not" he said, "let the death of so noble a Prince become a benefit to his enemies. Let us go together to the King of Harran, and make known to him the guilt of these wicked brethren. For surely the name of Codadad should live in story; but if you, whose honour he saved, now sink under your affliction his name perishes with you, and you have not retrieved your debt."

These words roused the Princess from her deep despondency; forming her resolution on the surgeon's advice, she arose instantly and prepared herself for the journey, and with such haste and diligence did she pursue her project, that within two days she and her companion arrived at the city of Harran.

Here strange news awaited them; for at all the caravanseri it was told how lately there had come to the city an exiled wife of the King, Princess Pirouzè by name, enquiring for news of her lost son; and how, asnow appeared, this son had already been under a feigned designation at his father's court, and after performing many exploits and deeds of heroism had disappeared none knew whither. Forty-nine sons had the King by different wives, but all these, it was declared, he would willingly put to death so only that Codadad might be restored to him.

She and her companion arrived at the city of Harran.

Now when the Princess of Deryabar heard this, she said, "I will go to the Queen Pirouzè and make known to her the fate of her son, and when we have wept together and drawn comfort from each other in our grief then we will go before the King, and demand vengeance on the murderers." But the surgeon said, "Have a care what you do; for if the Princes of Harran learn of your arrival, they will not rest till they have done to you as they did to your husband. Let us therefore proceed with secrecy, so as to ensure safety, and do you on no account let your presence here be known till the King has been thoroughly informed of the whole matter." Then leaving the Princess in a place discreetly chosen he went forth into the streets and began to direct his steps towards the palace. Presently he was met by a lady mounted upon a mule richly caparisoned, and behind her followed a great troop of guards and attendants. As she approached the populace ran out of their houses and stood in rows to see her go by, and when she passed all bowed down with their faces to the earth. The surgeon inquired of a beggar stand-near whether this was one of the King's wives. "Yes, brother," replied the beggar, "and the best of them all; for she is the mother of Prince Codadad, whom, now that he is lost, all hold in love and reverence. And thus each day she goes to the mosque to hear the prayers which the King has ordered for her son's safe return."

Seeing his course now clear the surgeon went and stood at the door of the mosque, waiting the Queen's departure, and when she came forth with all her attendants he plucked one of them by the sleeve and said to him, "If the Queen would have news of her son, Prince Codadad, let her send for the stranger who will be found waiting at the door of her palace." So, as soon as Pirouzè had returned to her apartments, the slave went in and gave his mistress the message. Then she sent in all haste and caused the surgeon to be brought before her. And the surgeon prostrated himself and said, "O Queen, let not the grief of the tidings which I bear be visited upon me but on them that were the cause of it." And she answered him, "Have peace, and say on!" So he told her, as has been here set forth, the full story of all the courage and prowess of Codadad, and of his generosity towards his brethren, also of his marriage to the Princess of Deryabar and of what followed after. But when he came to speak of the slaying of her son, the tender mother, as though receiving in her own body the strokes of the murderers fell forward upon the ground, and there for a while lay motionless without sign of life. When however the surgeon, aided by her women, had restored her to consciousness, then Pirouzè, putting aside all personal grief, set her mind upon the accomplishment of the duty which now lay before her. "Go instantly," she said, "and tell the Princess of Deryabar that the King will shortly receive her with all the honour due to her rank. As for yourself, be assured that your services will be remembered."

Hardly had the surgeon departed, when the King himself entered, and the sight of his Queen's deep affliction at once informed him that something dreadful must have occurred. "Alas," she cried, "our son no longer exists, nor is it even possible to pay to his body those last rites which were due to his rank and virtue, for stricken by treacherous hands and left to perish unprotected he has fallen a prey to wild beasts so that not a trace of him remains." She then proceeded to inform her husband of all the horrible circumstances which the surgeon had narrated.

But before she had ended the King became so transported with rage and grief that he could no longer delay the setting in motion of his just vengeance. Repairing in haste to the hall of audience, where courtiers and suitors stood waiting, he summoned to him his grand vizier with so much fury of countenance that all trembled for their lives.

"Go instantly," he cried, "arrest all the Princes, and convey them under a strong guard to the prison assigned for murderers!" The vizier, not daring to question an order so terribly uttered, went forth and fulfilled the King's command with all speed. On his return to the palace for the presentation of his report, a further order almost equally surprising awaited him. The King described to him a certain inn lying in a poor quarter of the city. "Go thither," said he, "take with you slaves and high attendants, a white mule from the royal stables, and a guard of honour, and bring hither with all the respect due to her rank the young Princess whom you shall find there."

And taking her hand he led her to the apartments of the Queen Pirouzè.

The vizier, with revived spirits, went forth to fulfil this second mission, so much more agreeable to him than the first; and presently there arose from the streets leading to the palace the acclamations of the populace because of the magnificence and splendour which announced the arrival of the unknown Princess. The King, as a token of respect, stood waiting at the palace gates to receive her, and taking her hand he led her to the apartments of the Queen Pirouzè. Here at the meeting of mother and wife a scene of the most tender and heart-rending affliction took place. The King himself was so moved by it that he had not the heart to refuse to them any request. So when they came and besought for the absent those funeral honours which under other circumstances would have been his due, he gave orders for a dome of marble to be erected on the plain by which the city of Harran lies surrounded. And with such speed was the work put in hand, and so large was the number of men employed upon it, that within three days the entire building was completed.

On the day following the obsequies began. All was done with the greatest solemnity and splendour. First came the King attended by his vizier and all the officers and lords of his palace; and entering the tomb, in which lay an effigy of Codadad, they seated themselves on carpets of mourning bordered with gold. Then followed the chiefs of the army mounted upon horses and bewailing the loss of him who had led them to victory; behind these came old men upon black mules, with long robes and flowing beards; and after these maidens on white horses, with heads unveiled, bearing in their hands baskets of precious stones. Now when these had approached and compassed the dome three times about, then the King rose up to speak the dismissal of the dead. Touching with his brow the tomb whereon the effigy lay, he cried in a loud voice, "O my dear son, O light of mine eyes, O joy that is lost to me for ever." After him all the lords and the chiefs and the elders came and prostrated themselves in like manner; and when the ceremony was ended the doors of the tomb were shut and all the people returned to the city.

Now after this there was prayer and fasting in the mosque for eight days, and on the ninth the King gave orders that the Princes were to be beheaded. But meanwhile the neighbouring powers, whose arms the King of Harran had defeated, as soon as they heard that Codadad was dead, banded themselves together in strong alliance, and with a great host began to advance upon the city. Then the King caused the execution to be postponed, and making a hasty levy of his forces went forth to meet the enemy in the open plain.

And there battle was joined with such valour and determination on both sides that for a time the issue remained doubtful. Nevertheless, because the men of Harran were fewer in number they began to be surrounded by their enemies; but at the very moment when all seemed lost they saw in the distance a large body of horsemen advancing at the charge; and while both combatants were yet uncertain of their purpose, these fell furiously and without warning upon the ranks of the allies, and throwing them into sudden disorder drove them in rout from the field.

After these, maidens on white horses, with heads unveiled, bearing in their hands baskets of precious stones.

With the success of their arms thus established the two leaders of the victorious forces advanced to meet each other in the presence of the whole army, and great was the joy and astonishment of the King when he discovered in the leader of the lately-arrived troop his lost son Codadad. The Prince, for his part, was equally delighted to find in his father's welcome the recognition for which he had yearned.

When the long transport of their meeting embrace was over, the Prince, as they began to converse, perceived with surprise how much was already known to the King of past events. "What?" he inquired, "has one of my brothers awakened to his guilt, and confessed that which I had meant should ever remain a secret?" "Not so," replied the King, "from the Princess of Deryabar alone have I learned the truth. For she it was who came to demand vengeance for the crime which your brothers would still have concealed."

At this unlooked-for news of the safety of the Princess and of her arrival at his father's court, Codadad's joy was beyond words, and greatly was it increased when he heard of his mother's reinstatement in the King's favour with the honour and dignity due to her rank. He now began to perceive how events had shaped themselves in his absence, and how the King had already become informed of the bond that existed between them. As for the rest of his adventures, together with the circumstance which had led to his disappearance and supposed death, they were soon explained. For when the Princess had left Codadad in her desperate search for aid, there chanced that way a travelling pedlar; and he, finding the youth apparently deserted and dying of his wounds, took pity on him, and placing him upon his mule bore him to his own house. There with medicinal herbs and simple arts unknown in the palaces of kings he had accomplished a cure which others would have thought impossible, so that in a short time Codadad's strength was completely restored. Thereupon the Prince impatient for reunion with those whom he loved, bestowed on the pedlar all the wealth that he possessed, and immediately set forth toward the city of Harran.

On the road news reached him of the fresh outbreak of hostilities followed by the invasion of his father's territory. Passing from village to village he roused and armed the inhabitants, and by the excellence of his example made such soldiers of them that they were able in the fortunate moment of their arrival to decide the issue of the conflict and give victory to the King's arms.

"And now, sire," said the Prince in conclusion, "I have only one request to make: since in the event all things have turned out so happily, I beg you to pardon my brothers in order that I may prove to them in the future how groundless were the resentment and jealousy that they felt toward me."

These generous sentiments drew tears from the King's eyes and removed from his mind all doubt as to the wisdom of the resolution he had been forming. Immediately before the assembled army he declared Codadad his heir, and, as an act of grace to celebrate his son's return, gave orders for the Princes to be released. He then led Codadad with all speed to the palace, where Pirouzè and her daughter-in-law were anxiously awaiting them.

In the joy of that meeting the Prince and his wife were repaid a thousandfold for all the griefs and hardships they had undergone: and their delight in each other's society remained so great that in all the world no happiness has been known to equal it. The Princes half died of shame when the means by which their pardon had been procured was revealed to them; but before long the natural insensibility of their characters reasserted itself and they recovered.